BLACK BEAD

BOOK ONE OF THE BLACK BEAD CHRONICLES

Other Books in the Black Bead Chronicles:

Welcome to the adventure — Lakey

BLACK BEAD

BOOK ONE OF THE BLACK BEAD CHRONICLES

by
J.D. Lakey

Book Cover & Illustrations by Dylan Drake

Black Bead

ISBN-13: 978-0-692-60947-7
ISBN-10: 0-692-60947-4

Book Website:
www.JDLakey.com

Contact:
info@JDLakey.com

Book Design by:
www.WaywordAuthorServices.com
www.DylanDrakeDesignInc.com

Printed in the U.S.A
Second Edition, January 2016

For
All the children of my Heart

Planet Tearmann
The High Reaches

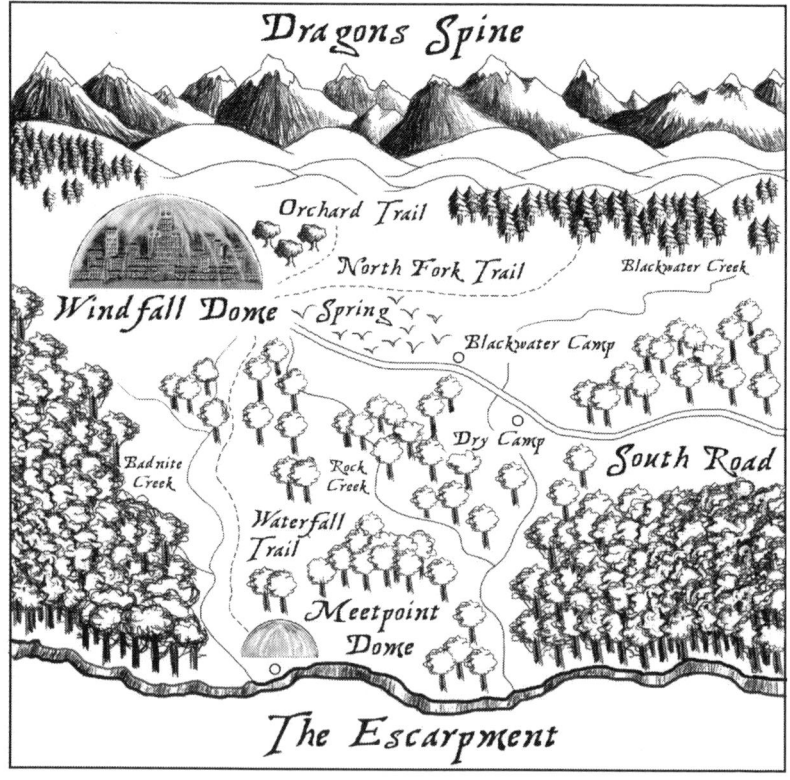

The real danger
When creating a weapon
Meant to destroy your enemies
Is not that you will fail
But that you will succeed
Beyond all expectations

The Book of Mysteries;
The Living Thread, 12.37.15

CONTENTS

Chapter One

Cheobawn looked up from her playthings and waited. Something had been stalking her in the shadows at the back of her mind since dawn and now it drew near. The thing stank of unnamed yearnings, unfulfilled wishes, and a hunger so deep it made her feel hollow inside. She counted its steps under her breath. One. Two. Three. On six, three young boys turned the corner, sauntered casually down the walkway that fronted the playground fence, and stopped at the gates.

"Ten," whispered Cheobawn, watching them intently. Something about them piqued her interest. Other seekers had come. More than a few. These boys seemed different, somehow.

Was it their outer appearance that caught at her imagination? The boys were dressed like every other child in the village, in basic tunic and shorts, though these three made an attempt at looking presentable, with their damp hair pasted back against their skulls and their clothes freshly laundered, the creases still sharp from the hot irons used by the Mothers in the laundry.

Yet it was their clothes that seemed to set them apart from other boys. Cheobawn calmed her thoughts and let the details of the scene wash through her mind, wishing to solve this puzzle.

The Mothers never threw anything away if it still had use, especially clothing, since the process of turning dyes and yarns into fabric was labor intensive and relegated to the long dark days of midwinter. Clothes outgrown were simply returned to the communal stores, to be recycled and reissued to the next child in line. Time and use faded the natural dyes. The youngest children were invariably dressed in motley shades of pale.

These three boys, on the other hand, had somehow convinced the Mothers in charge of the stores to give them three almost identical outfits whose dyes were still rich and bright. Their multi-pocketed shorts were the same brown, their tunics an identical shade of green, no mean feat when one considered the vagaries of the weaving and dyeing processes.

On the surface, the uniformity of their appearance seemed prideful and vain, but Cheobawn found the effect comforting somehow. In a scuffle or an all out brawl, she imagined, it would be an advantage to tell at a glance who was friend and who was foe. Why males enjoyed solving their problems with their fists was a different puzzle that she would save for another day.

The troop of boys did not immediately enter the school yard. Instead they loitered, milling about in that jittery, wound up way universal to all little boys. It always reminded her of nervous herd animals with the smell of leopard up their noses. She did not need her psi skills to guess their purpose. Their furtive glances were drawn to Megan. The tall, slender girl, busy leading a dozen little girls in a complicated game of Dancing Molly, did not notice the boys right away.

Cheobawn slid further back into her favorite hiding place.

The long thin leaves of the densely packed tubegrass curved over her head, casting her bower into deep shade. From here she could watch the world, safely unnoticed. From here she could watch the watchers.

The boys argued. It was a brief, intense storm on the ambient, quickly quashed by the leader, the loser sucking his unhappiness back behind the walls of his mind. Cheobawn sighed in relief, grateful for their self control. Such was the life in a village full of witches. One learned early to guard one's thoughts.

Perhaps sensing the brief storm, Megan looked up and noticed them for the first time. She paused for a moment, her face betraying nothing, before turning back to her duties. Pretending indifference, she immersing herself in play with Cheobawn's classmates, but her voice became too bright, too loud, too forced. Cheobawn grimaced, embarrassed for her friend. There would be no advantage to be had in the ensuing negotiations if the boys knew their interest was returned in kind.

Cheobawn had seen this all before, this awkward dance. As often as she watched it play out, it still puzzled her. It seemed to her that more things were going on under the surface than just picking partners. She had asked Da to explain it. He said six-year-olds were not meant to know certain things and she would understand it better when she got older. Cheobawn doubted this.

Would the boys gather the courage to cross the line into Megan's domain?

Bored, Cheobawn turned her attention back to her play. She placed another pebble carefully along the finger wide roads she had etched in the dust. The roads wound through a miniature world made of rocks, wooden toys, flowers and bits of stick and weeds. Cheobawn put her cheek down in the dust to see what the world looked like from the pebble's point of view.

The gate squeaked open, catching at her attention. The leader had found his courage at last. He crossed towards Megan while his mates hung back near the gate. Cheobawn smiled and lifted her head to watch the drama. This was not the first demi-Pack that had come hunting Megan. It would probably not be the last. Megan had very particular standards.

The boy, Tam was his name, stopped a few paces from Megan and bowed politely. There was an unconscious grace in the way he moved that made even this formality seem less an act of subservience and more like the first step in a well choreographed weapons form. Cheobawn listened to the ambient, curious about this strange boy in spite of herself. His hunger infected his mind, preceding him in waves. He wanted so much more than what the world was willing to give him. It was a sentiment she could understand.

Hope was not a thing she usually allowed in her heart, having been disappointed far too often but there it was, filling her and making the world brighter with its promise.

She knew of Tam. She had never had any harsh dealings with him, which already put him a notch above most of the boys of the village, whose curiosity could turn cruel. The beads of his omeh, barely visible above the neckline of his tunic, marked him as a son of the Waterwall tribe. His midnight black hair, so different from Home Dome's sandy haired denizens, proclaimed his eastern tribe origins.

She remembered the caravan that had brought him, along with the handful of seven-year-old boys acquired that year from the Eastern Trade Fair. It had been three years ago. She had marked it in her mind because the men had staggered into the village nearly frozen, the pack animals driven close to death in the mad race to get down out of the passes before an unseasonable winter storm made the high mountain roads impassable. The Mothers, the fiasco of her Choosingday only weeks old and fresh in their minds, had blamed her Bad Luck for the odd weather just as they had blamed her Bad Luck for every mishap and change in their fortunes since.

Cheobawn did the math. That would mean Tam was over ten years old now. Technically, by village counting, that made him the same age as Megan, though Megan would not be ten for another few months.

A squabble broke out between two little girls about the finer points of Dancing Molly, drowning out anything Tam might have been saying. Megan broke it up with a soft word and a group hug and then rose to her full height, giving Tam a wintry stare. Since she was half a head taller than Tam, this made her gaze seem almost regal. Tam did not flinch under that look as Cheobawn had seen other boys do. Instead he returned her gaze and tried again, saying something with an eloquent gesture of his fine boned hands. Cheobawn admired him for his persistence.

"Are you the one? Please be the one," she whispered softly to herself.

She watched them talk, her imagination filling in the conversion that she could not hear. Tam needed an Ear, that was obvious. All the ten-year-old boys with dreams of leading a Pack needed an Ear. Without a girl gifted with the psi skills needed to keep a Pack safely out of harms way, they could not make an independent foray outside Home Dome. Without an Ear, the demi-Packs went outside only as baggage on some other Pack's foray, like the babies, the old, and the pregnant women. There was no honor in it and more importantly, any points won while on a mission went to the alpha commander of the lead Pack, not to the tag-along demi-Packs.

Megan answered Tam. Tam frowned and tried to argue. Megan folded her arms over her flat chest, a sure sign that she could not be persuaded. She spoke again, shaking her short, sun bleached curls away from her face.

Cheobawn dropped her eyes and studied her fingers where they lay buried in the cool earth. Here it comes, she thought sadly. Megan had stated her terms. Tam would argue and eventually say no. The boys always said no. Cheobawn sighed. One day, quite soon, Megan would follow her own internal needs and say yes. She needed a Pack as much as the boys needed a Little Mother to play Ear. Someday, soon, Cheobawn would be alone.

Cheobawn let her mind wander away, sinking it deep into the roots of the mountain underneath her hands, letting the cool darkness there ease the ache of her sorrow.

It was a surprise then, when a pair of shadows moved to block out the bright light streaming through the dome high over their heads. Cheobawn looked up into a pair of curious hazel eyes set in a kind face.

"Hello, Little Mother," Tam said.

"Ch'che, this is Tam. He wants to ask you something," Megan said, smiling encouragingly from behind Tam's back.

Tam studied her. Cheobawn watched his eyes slide over the black bead set in her own omeh and then return to her face to meet her gaze. His expression did not betray his thoughts. Her estimation of him rose one more notch. Most people flinched from the implications of her black bead. His omeh, like Megan's, already held a handful of honors, no mean feat for someone so young. Cheobawn's omeh held nothing but her tribe designation and the hated black bead. With all those honors, he could have had his pick of any eligible girl in the village yet he came seeking Megan, who came burdened with a Black Bead child that she would not abandon.

Tam squatted down to Cheobawn's level to speak to her. She did not care if the move was calculated or unconscious; it made him less intimidating. Perhaps, she thought to herself, I just might like you. She returned his gaze solemnly.

"My Pack needs an Ear, Little Mother. Megan says she'll come but you have to come along, too. What do you say? Please say yes."

Cheobawn blinked, surprised by the strange emotions those words triggered inside her. People did not have to be nice or polite to her when her Truemother was not around, so they generally were not. She glanced at Megan, who nodded, an excited little smile playing at the corners of her mouth.

Cheobawn looked down at her miniature world and pointed at one pebble after another.

"Stinging spiders, buzzy hive, fuzzy gang, fenelk, bhotta den, treebear," Cheobawn recited. Then she pointed at the toys and flowers and the weed stalks. "Bloodstones, honeypots, hoppers, bog apples, fernhens, silk spiders."

A blank expression crossed Tam's face. At least he had the grace not to laugh out loud.

"That's a nice game, Little Mother, but I want to go outside. Outside?," he said the last loudly, as if she was hard of hearing.

Megan giggled. Cheobawn scowled at both of them and reached out to brush away her designs. Megan stooped quickly, catching her wrist before she could do too much damage.

"Don't be silly. He didn't understand your model. You have to be patient with boys," saying the last as if that explained so much of life's puzzles.

"Model? Map? That's a map?" Tam asked, a light dawning in his brain.

"Do not be fooled by her size or her age. Amabel knew what she was doing when she made Ch'che. Mora did not want just any ordinary truedaughter. Now pay attention. This mound of sand," Megan explained, pointing, "is the Home Dome. Those flowers are the gates. The lines are roads and trails. The rocks are bad things. The toys and such are good things. North on the model is north in the real world. Do you need her to repeat the list?" Megan asked, testing him.

"No, wait," Tam said, studying the things etched in the dust. After a moment he looked up and met Cheobawn's steady gaze. His next question surprised her. "Did you make this for me? How did you know I was coming?"

Cheobawn snorted in disgust. Demi-Packs, despite all their lessons, seemed to view the psi abilities of Little Mothers in a singularly egocentric way.

"She makes them every morning. It helps her keep track of things," Megan explained. "Go ahead. Ask her something else."

"Like what?"

"Belief takes trust," Cheobawn said cryptically, moving a stone.

"Huh?"

"She wants you to test her Ears," Megan translated patiently.

"A test? Oh," he mused, thinking for a moment. "Alright. Say I wanted to go five clicks north of Home Dome along the Orchard Road. What is out there?"

Cheobawn rose up onto her hands and knees and very carefully extended a winding line and then put a handful of rocks just off the left hand side of the trail.

"Dubeh leopards," she said. "A mom and her cubs."

Tam stared at the little pile of stones and then looked back at her, obviously thinking hard.

"Mora gets all the field reports every morning. Who is to say she did not read them and is just drawing from memory?" he suggested to Megan.

Cheobawn smiled slyly at him, daring him to believe that.

"Do not torment him, Ch'che," the older girl scolded. To Tam she said, "The reports go to the office of the First Mother, not to her living quarters."

"My truemother mother keeps her comscreen locked against me. Every time I figure out her pass code, she changes it," Cheobawn sniffed in annoyance.

Tam studied them both, trying to see if the two girls were playing some sort of game at his expense. Megan blinked innocently at him. Cheobawn continued moving the pieces in her miniature world. He looked down, distracted by the movement, perhaps wishing he had paid more attention to her descriptions of the markers.

Cheobawn moved a pair of stones and decided to take pity on him.

"Fenelk mother and her yearling calf," she said, tapping the pebbles to the west of the sand mound. "She smells the fuzzy gang and moves up the mountain, putting distance between herself and them. She need not worry. Fuzzies have full bellies. They found the treebear's den last night and will not eat again for days," Cheobawn assured him.

"How does she do that?" Tam asked. "They never told me that the Ears could be this accurate."

"That's nothing," Megan said, purposefully ignoring his question. "Current ambient is easy. Watch this. She's amazing. Ch'che, show me the mountain at day's end."

Cheobawn put her hand out and then paused. The day slipped away from her and fell into disarray. How curious. This had never happened to her before. The days of the Windfall tribe were as predictable as the sunrise. She chewed on her bottom lip and pondered the source of such uncertainty.

A thought came to her from out of nowhere. Since she was obviously about to go outside, out beyond the edges of the well patrolled perimeter of the village, the presence of her future self altered the map. The more she tried to see the future, her own future, the more chaotic it became.

"Ch'che?" Megan prompted, concerned.

"Well, that was impressive," commented Tam, his voice dripping with sarcasm.

"Shhh," Megan hissed. "Ch'che, is there something wrong?"

"I am out there. All possibilities exist in me," Cheobawn said vaguely, trying to sort out the infinite number of futures running through her head.

"Huh?" said Megan.

"You are one spooky little kid, did you know that?" commented Tam.

Cheobawn stood up and brushed the dirt off her grubby knees. This was exciting. She wanted to hurry up and find out what her future self was up to.

Tam and Megan did not move. They squatted in the dust and stared up at her with their mouths open.

"Well? Are we going outside or not?" Cheobawn asked impatiently.

"Unh," grunted Tam, shaking his head, "Sure, why not?"

Cheobawn grinned at them both and stepped around them to saunter over to the gate. The two boys eyed her uncertainly and then looked up as Tam approached.

"Connor, Alain, this is Megan and Cheobawn. They are coming with us," Tam said by way of introductions. Alain's

omeh marked him as Firewalker tribe. She did not need to see
his collar to know this. His auburn hair, flashing coppery in the
bright light, had been a dead give away. Cheobawn thought his
hair beautiful despite the Mothers' amusement. Flash without
substance, Amabel had sniffed in disdain, but Amabel was not
prone to frivolity and perhaps found the bright colors not suited
to the weight of the office of Maker of the Living Thread.

Mora, behind closed doors, had been amused as well, but
here stood Alain, traded one for one, made Son of the Heart to
replace a Son of the Flesh, proof perhaps that Mothers could be
seduced by more than logic when it came to picking the future
husbands of the dome.

Connor, the smallest of the boys, was Waterwall tribe, just
like Tam. He was a shorter, rougher boned version of Tam's
golden skinned darkness. She did not remember him from Tam's
caravan, so he surely must be younger, by a year or two. He did
not have as many honor beads as Tam or Alain but he was still
young enough for that not to matter.

The one called Alain stared at the beaded collar around her
own neck.

"But she's . . . She's the . . . " he sputtered, groping for a word
that did not offend.

Cheobawn kept her hands by her side, resisting the instinctive
urge to cover the large black bead set in the center of her omeh.
Instead, she lifted her chin proudly, as if to offer them a better
view of her collar.

" . . . an excellent Ear," Tam finished the sentence, glaring at
Alain as he held the gate open for the girls.

"Why do we need two girls?" whined the one named Connor.
"The rules only say we need one."

"Because I can outrun you, out climb you, out wrestle you,

and beat you at bladed sticks," growled Megan, pushing her face close to Connor's. "If she does not go, I do not go. Got a problem with that?"

Connor looked up at her with a dark scowl on his face, obviously wanting to take her up on that challenge. The boy had a suicidal streak, thought Cheobawn, or maybe he had not seen Megan on the skirmish floor. Tam punched him in the shoulder, redirecting his attention to where it needed to be.

"We need them both. They are a team like we are a team. Cheobawn is six and doesn't qualify as a Pack guide. We need Megan to get her past the gate guards," Tam said firmly. "Besides, Megan has been outside the dome a million times on harvester forays and knows the terrain close to the dome by heart. Let's go."

Alain opened his mouth to object but Tam gave him no opportunity. Instead, the Pack leader pivoted on his heel and marched down the promenade back the way they had come. The others had no choice but to follow.

Chapter Two

Tam led his odd little procession across the Central Plaza. Cheobawn watched the faces of the people they passed. There were stares yet no one stopped them or yelled at Cheobawn to get on home. By the time they reached the Pack Hall, she started to relax a little.

Phillius, Mora's Third Prime, sat dozing behind the desk in the common room. He opened one eye as they entered. The appearance of Cheobawn in the group wiped the bored expression from his face. He sat up abruptly, a half uttered oath on his lips.

Tam planted himself in front of the desk and opened his mouth to say something. Phillius stopped him with a look and a wave of his hand. Tam pressed his lips together tensely and waited as the Third Prime touched the comscreen in front of him and waited for a response.

"What?" the harassed sounding voice of the Hayrald, the First Prime, snapped out of the speaker.

"Sent Tam out to fill out his Pack. You'll never guess who he brought back." Phillius said brightly.

"By the Goddess, Phil, I do not have time for games," Hayrald growled. "Tell me why I should care?"

"He came back with Megan and Cheobawn."

There was a long silence. Cheobawn held her breath.

"I'll get back to you," Cheobawn's Da said tensely and the com went dead. Cheobawn bit her lower lip. This surely could not be good. She fully expected Hayrald to come storming through the door in the next few minutes.

Phillius looked at Tam and shook his head.

"You are one hard-headed boy, Tam Waterwall. Can you never go at life along the easy road?" Phillius asked not unkindly.

"Easy is boring, Father," Tam said, his bravado not entirely convincing to Cheobawn's ears. "Nobody ever became great by taking the easy road."

"Yeah, but they managed to stay alive. Do you have a death wish? Hayrald will skin you personally if anything happens to her."

Tam frowned. He set his gaze on a spot on the wall behind the older man's left shoulder and drew himself up to his full height.

"I know what I am doing, sir," he said stubbornly.

"No," Phillius said firmly, "I don't think you do, but you surely are about to find out."

Tam did not choose to argue further. He fell into a stony silence.

"Phillius, you there?" Hayrald's voice crackled over the comlink. "Take me off speaker and put in an earbud."

Phillius touched the screen, opened the top drawer of his desk and rummaged around for a few moments. His search yielded results of a dubious nature. Phillius brushed the crumbs off a rather crushed looking earbud and shoved it into his ear.

"Go ahead," he said and then listened for a moment. The children watched his face as it went through a rapid series of emotions and then settled on no emotion at all. Cheobawn recognized that look. She had grown up sitting at Mora's knee, watching the men of the village accept the decrees handed down from the chair of the First Mother. Here it was, on Phillius's face, the look of someone swallowing their dismay like bitter medicine.

Hayrald had not come for her, to drag her back to school. That meant only one thing. Hayrald had talked to her Truemother. She recognized the nuances in Phillius's manner. Mora's instructions had not been well received. Cheobawn prepared herself for the worst.

"Yes, sir," Phillius said finally. He took the earbud out, tossed it back where it came from and slammed the drawer shut with a little more force than was necessary. Then he started keying in information on his screen as he rattled off instructions.

"Alright. I am putting your names down under provisional Pack. You can change your status if and when you decide to go permanent, but I highly recommend you stay temporary for at least a year. No sense rushing into anything until you get a little bit older and your heads get screwed on a little tighter. Four man team, Tam is the alpha male. Megan, the alpha female. Who you got earmarked for beta male?" When there was no response, Phillius paused and stared at the children, waiting.

"We're a five man Pack," Tam corrected.

"No," Phillius said patiently, "you are a four plus one. She," he pointed at Cheobawn, "is six years old and cannot be put on a roster for two more years. She also comes with her own set of rules. Under-agers are not allowed more than two clicks from the dome. If you encounter hostiles, you will not engage.

Got that? No engagement. Period. Retreat and return to Home Dome. Is that understood?"

Tam ground his teeth together and glowered at no one in particular.

"What's that? I didn't hear you." Phillius said loudly.

"Ye'sir," the boys chorused together without much enthusiasm.

"Now, who is to be your Second and who is the Third?" he asked again.

"Alain is beta, I guess, because he's oldest," Tam ventured. Connor squawked in protest. Tam quelled his outburst with a glare.

"Fine," Phillius said, as he keyed the information into his form. "Pick up your tools and weapons at the weapons locker. Don't forget to check with the Weapons Master. Do not lose your tools. Return them cleaned and undamaged or there will be dire consequences. Where is your foray form?"

"Uh," Tam grunted, looking over at Megan. She sighed in exasperation and grabbed an empty form and a stylus from a stack on the corner of the desk. She turned on her heel and crossed the room to the row of seats set against the near wall. The Pack followed her.

"That's alright," yelled Phillius after them, "Take your time. I've got all day. Maybe the sun will set and you won't have to bother going outside."

Cheobawn's head was spinning. She could hardly believe it. Her Da was letting her go. More importantly, Mora was allowing it. The world was so full of surprises. She floated across the room, barely aware of her feet touching the floor.

Megan unfolded the form and laid it flat on the low table in front of chairs. The boys gathered round. Cheobawn squeezed in past Alain and sat next to Megan, snuggling up close to see what was printed on the paper. Most of the paper was covered with a map of some kind. Words and numbers and lines of every color and weight swirled and coiled in upon themselves. None of it made any sense at first glance. Then she spotted the black circle in the center of the paper labeled Home Dome. She leaned in closer, studying the drawing. If you ignored most of the swirly twirly stuff and just looked at the black lines, it became intimately familiar. This was her miniature world, only instead of being modeled in dust, someone had committed it to paper.

They did not teach map reading to six-year-olds although she knew maps. A beautiful map was tacked to the wall in her classroom. It had little cartoons of mountains covered with cartoon trees and cartoon rock jumpers, with cartoon domes strung like beads in the spaces between the mountains and the edge of the world. She liked to trace the roads that connected the other domes to the Windfall dome, reading the names of each village, imagining how magical it would be to live someplace so far away.

The map on the foray form was different. Familiar lines marked West Road, Waterfall Trail, Orchard Trail and East Trail that split around a ridge and formed North Fork Trail and South Road. The paler lines curled and coiled in a confusing way until she realized they marked the places she knew to be high ground and ridge lines. She puzzled over the lines that formed a pattern of chevrons and then decided they matched the ravines in the model in her head.

The map had more secrets. Scattered across the paper were little numbered boxes of various colors with a key along the side to decipher their meaning. Cheobawn studied it intently, enraptured by the cleverness and precision of the mind that had invented it. The key indicated that a red box with the number nine represented dubeh leopards. She looked back at the map, letting her eye follow the black line labeled Orchard Trail up the page. A pleased smile touched her face. There was a red box at five clicks just as she had told Tam. The dubeh leopard's den was known to the Elders.

"Where do you want to go?" Megan asked.

"Two clicks," moaned Connor. "Where is the fun in that? I thought the whole point of a foray was to get out from under the thumb of all the adults. We're going to be bumping into patrols every time we turn around."

"What do you say, Cheobawn?" Tam asked softly, ignoring his newly designated Third. "Shall we show Connor a good time?"

"Why are you asking her?" Connor snorted.

Tam punched him in the shoulder. Connor scowled and rubbed the doubly injured appendage as Tam moved to put his body between Cheobawn and Phillius before he spoke again.

"Quiet," he hissed. "Do you want everyone to know our business? You guys keep your mouths shut and follow my lead." Alain and Connor exchanged looks over the top of Tam's head. Connor raised an eyebrow. Alain shrugged.

"Cheobawn!" hissed Tam, drawing her attention away from the interesting play of power amongst the boys. She looked down at the map and cocked her head. It took her a moment but she managed to superimposed her own mental picture of the world on top of the curling lines. Fun, she thought. Something happy answered her. She put her finger on the spot that made her insides bubble with laughter.

"Too far. That's five clicks, at least," Alain said, shaking his head.

Cheobawn moved her finger back toward the dome to a line labeled North Fork Trail.

"If we walk fast, no one will know that we ever went where we should not," she suggested softly.

"Wow," Connor breathed, "and I thought girls would make things more boring."

"I am all up for a good adventure, but if we get in trouble, no one will know where to find us," Alain stated, a worried frown on his face.

"No trouble," Cheobawn said with absolute certainty.

"What a load of dung. Why are we listening to her?" Connor asked. Tam lifted his fist. Connor put his hand over his shoulder and shied away. Tam turned to Megan.

"What does your Ear say?" he asked her. Megan cocked her head to the side and listened, her eyes gone distant. Then she shrugged.

"The way is clear now. No imminent threats," she said. Tam gave Alain a smug look and then turned to Cheobawn.

"Show the closest trouble, wee bit," Tam suggested.

Cheobawn took the stylus from Megan and drew seven squares on different spots on the map. Then, consulting the key, she filled in the numbers. All were more than a click from their intended path.

"How do . . . nobody can do that. Is this some kind of trick?" Alain sputtered.

"Let's go find out," Tam said, a sly smile on his face.

Alain and Connor slid suspicious looks from Tam to Megan to Cheobawn and then back again, trying to figure out who was conning whom.

"Boys," Megan sniffed in annoyance, growing out of patience with their squabbles. She took the stylus from Cheobawn and drew a slightly serpentine line from the dome symbol to the spot just this side of the two click mark on the North Fork Trail. Then she filled in the empty lines below the map.

"I am calling this a foraging mission, with no particular goal in mind. There and back again, gleaning what we can find. Any objections?" she asked.

If they had any, the look she gave the boys made them think twice about voicing them.

Tam considered the map for a moment, thinking hard.

"Alright. This is how it's going to go. We get outside the eyesight of the dome guards and then double time it to the spot Cheobawn picked, have our fun and then glean on our way back. Nobody expects full baskets on a first time foray and the areas near the dome are always harvested first, so we can say the pickings were lean."

Cheobawn beamed in delight. The plan was brilliant. Tam was rapidly becoming her favorite person in the whole world, after her Da and Megan, of course. Tam looked around the group. Connor and Alain nodded.

"Fine," he said, grabbing the form and returning to the desk. He handed it to Phillius, who read it with amusement.

"Wow," said Phillius dryly, "an oldma could cover more territory. I take back what I said about the hard road, Tam."

The newly formed Pack's alpha male returned the older man's gaze calmly, his face betraying nothing. Cheobawn cocked her head and listened. She liked what she felt coming from the Pack leader's head. There was a cleverness and a confidence that comforted her. She began to relax a little more. Trusting Tam's judgment could become dangerously easy.

Phillius looked back at the map and stiffened. Cheobawn bit her lip. It suddenly occurred to her that her boxed numbers did not belong on a foray form and that surely Phillius would suspect who had put them there. The Coven chose to ignore her gifts but the Fathers were painfully aware of them and tried to protect her from her own folly whenever possible. When Phillius lifted his gaze, his eyes found Cheobawn. She smiled, trying to appear the picture of innocence.

Phillius considered her, a worried scowl on his brow. The children held their breath. Despite Mora and Hayrald's instructions, Phillius had final say on all forays while he sat at this desk. After an endless moment, the Third Prime sighed in resignation and finished filling out his foray report. It seemed to take forever. Finally, he stopped and handed the map back to Tam. Pinning them with a glare, he pulled a blue medallion out of his pocket. He held it up. They all stared at it as if it were a magical talisman from a fairytale.

"Give this tag to the gate guard and take the red one he gives you. Do not lose your tag. It is the only way to keep track of who is in and who is out of the dome. Gleaner baskets can be found in the Pantries. Remember everything you have been taught and don't do anything stupid. Mess this up and you all will be staying in, doing drills, until the snow melts next spring, got that?"

"Ye'sir," the Pack barked smartly, almost dancing in anticipation.

"Go on, get out of here, before I change my mind," Phillius growled, handing the blue tag to Tam.

Tam snatched it up and herded his Pack out into the diffused sunlight.

Out on the promenade, Alain leapt into the air and whooped like a banshee, coming down with a grin stretching from ear to ear. Tam grinned back at him as he grabbed Connor in a headlock and tousled his hair. A jostling match ensued amongst the boys until Megan cleared her throat loudly.

"Uh, right," Tam said, breaking away and becoming more serious. "Let's go. Daylight's wasting."

Chapter Three

The gaggle of children crossed the Central Plaza again, their pace somewhere between a jog and a joyous skip. At the Pantry they sorted through the backpacks and baskets hanging on the wall by the door, all the while trying to stay out from underfoot of the day's kitchen detail who were busy gathering ingredients for the communal evening meal from the bins, baskets and boxes that lined every surface in the room. When everyone had a gleaning basket, Tam went from child to child making sure of the fit, testing shoulder straps and waist straps, making adjustments when needed. He was set to lead them back outside when he stopped suddenly.

"Wait here. I forgot something," he said. Turning, he ran back into the bowels of the immense storage room. He returned minutes later, his arms heaped high with tins of trail rations, plus five full water skins hung over one shoulder.

"I nearly forgot," he said with an apologetic shrug, handing them out. "We will miss the midday meal while we are outside."

Suitably provisioned, they left the Pantry and raced each other back across the square to the weapons warehouse. The children tumbled through the door, breathless with laughter.

The duty of weapons master had fallen on Zeff this day. He was her favorite oldpa. She loved that he wore his silver hair long and pulled back in a knot at the back of his head. Few Fathers lived to get the silver in their hair. Cheobawn thought it made him look elegant and wise. It certainly set him apart from all the other Fathers who kept their hair cut close for convenience.

The old man looked up, smiling. Then he caught site of Cheobawn's short frame in their midst. The smile faded to be replaced with an intense stillness. Cheobawn watched him, wondering if males had psi abilities that they did not reveal to the Mothers for surely Zeff was listening to his own personal ambient. Cheobawn held her breath and waited for the scolding. It did not come, though it was apparent that Zeff had much he wanted to say. Instead, the old man grunted and held out his hand.

"Let's see your tag," he said.

Tam held it up but did not relinquish it, as if it were too precious to be risked in strange hands.

"Phillius already checked with Hayrald," Tam said in a rush, trying to belay any more arguments. "We are a four plus one, in the records under temporary Pack."

Zeff met Cheobawn's eyes, a doubtful look on his face. Cheobawn gave him an tremulous smile, wishing with all her heart that he would put away whatever reservations he was feeling. Mora could not keep her locked up in the dark for the rest of her life and the village Fathers could not protect her from her own fate, as much as they wished to. The Pack held their breath and waited.

"Fine," Zeff said at last. "Everyone go get your tools and come back here."

Alain headed towards the rack of short swords. Tam grabbed him by the arm and steered them all over to the rack of bladed sticks. While nicely suited for cutting down hard to reach fruits and nuts, the sticks turned into deadly weapons in well-trained hands. It was the first weapons form every child learned.

Cheobawn, too short for the long weapon, went over to another rack and picked up a gleaner's hook. The short staff, meant for harvesting wild grain, had a small, sickle shaped blade on one end.

"Belt knives?" Alain suggested eagerly Megan and Cheobawn exchanged looks. They all carried pocket knives. A belt knife seemed a bit much.

"Simple is better," commented Cheobawn to no one in particular.

"We have to travel fast. Do we really need the extra weight?" Megan added.

"One hunting knife, in case we have to field dress a carcass. Alain, you are the biggest. You carry it," Tam decided.

Megan and Cheobawn exchanged amused glances. The likelihood of this lot bringing down a game animal on their first foray was laughably non-existent.

The ever-hopeful Alain grinned and scampered across the room to the knife drawers. He joined them at the counter as Zeff began to enter their weapons list into the form on his screen. Tam looked down as Alain slipped a ten inch blade onto his belt.

"Really?" Tam asked. Alain grinned at him, his good mood irrepressible.

Zeff rattled off the rules, almost identical to Phillius's instructions.

At the end he pointed at Cheobawn.

"Littlest in the center of the group at all times. The big cats pick the easy prey off the front and back first. Pay attention. The mountain gets to keep what it takes. Remember that."

"Ye'sir," they chorused solemnly.

Zeff looked like he wanted to say more. They waited.

"By the Mother!" he growled, waving them out. "Get going. There's nothing I can say that you won't learn the hard way on your own. Scat!"

They tripped over each other's heels trying to get out the door first.

"Zeff. Always so cheerful and positive," Connor said with a snort.

"He worries," Cheobawn said.

"Why jinx us," Megan fretted, "by thinking only the worst things?"

Cheobawn thought of the bright giggly place in the middle of the woods and laughed.

"No worries, no trouble, just fun," she assured them, twirling her hook in her fingers. Connor and Alain laughed, trying to mimic her moves with their sticks.

Tam squinted at Megan.

"Should I ask her what she knows or just wait and be surprised?"

"It never gets any clearer if you push her. I have found it is best to be patient," she said.

"Patience," agreed Cheobawn, with a spin of her hook.

Tam smiled but he tapped the spinning blades down out of the air with his own and shooed them all towards the East Gate.

They had one more stop to make before they could exit Home Dome. The East Gate's changing room stood just a dozen strides from the gate. It contained stockpiles of communal work clothing used only for exterior forays. The leather aprons, coats, riding chaps, bonnets and wide brimmed straw hats hung neatly on hooks. Gloves, hats and outer wear of every sort were stored in vermin proof chests. The room smelled of cedar and soap and leather polish. Cheobawn sniffed deeply. There was so much promise in that smell. For the rest of her life that smell would remind her of the excitement of freedom under bright skies.

They shed their village slippers, replacing them with the more sturdy wayfaring boots well padded with felted liners. Cheobawn found a pair of boot liners that fit her small feet. It took a good amount of hunting to find boots in her size. By the time she was suitably shod, the Pack had found its way over to the gaiter bin and within minutes were lacing up the reinforced leather thorn shields on forearms and calves.

Cheobawn picked through the communal bins, looking for thorn guards that would fit her small form. She was starting to feel a little grumpy. The day they became an official Pack they would be able to requisition their own personal gear. As a temporary Pack they were reduced to wearing the well used castoffs of the older Packs. That day could not come soon enough, thought Cheobawn, her frustration growing.

She stamped her foot. None of the gaiters fit her. This was pointless. She was too small. She watched sadly while the rest of her Pack tightened up the laces on their leather armor and headed for the door, chatting excitedly.

Tam counted noses and paused, looking back.

"Hey, wee bit. What's the problem?"

"Nothing fits," Cheobawn said forlornly.

"She needs gaiters," Alain said, stating the obvious. "This is supposed to be a gleaner mission into the deep bush."

"Can't she do without?" Megan asked anxiously. "It's not like we actually mean to glean."

Tam shook his head, a worried look on his face.

"Everyone else gets to dress up but me. I want to look like a warrior, too," Cheobawn protested, her lip trembling.

Tam stared at her sad little face and then looked around the shed in desperation. His eyes lit on the storage chests set against the side wall.

"Come on. There might be something we can use." He ran his fingers down the inventory lists pinned to the outside of each of the chests.

"Dusters. Parkas. Snowsuits. Mukluks. Ah ha! Mittens and hats," he crowed triumphantly. Tam hit the release button on the lid. It barely had time to unseal and swing open before Tam was digging under the top layer of aromatic cedar boughs. He seemed to be looking for something very specific as his quest took him deeper and deeper into the box. When it seemed he must have surely dug to the bottom and only his legs were visible, he let out a muffled cry of success.

Cheobawn giggled at the piece of anatomy he presented to them. Megan hushed her.

Tam emerged from the chest covered in dried needles, holding up a wad of white cloth, a triumphant grin on his face.

"Woolsey neck scarves," Tam crowed.

"It's the height of summer," Megan reminded him.

"No, wait, this will be so awesome it just might set a trend with the other kids. Trust me," he said.

He sat Cheobawn down on a bench. Going back to the gaiter bin, he grabbed an armful of extremely large leather gaiters.

These he stripped of their leather laces which he brought back to Cheobawn. Taking a woolsey scarf, he began wrapping Cheobawn's calf, starting just below her ankle on the outside of her boot and working upward. Tucking the ends in, he picked up a long leather cord. This he folded double so that he could loop it under the heel of her hard soled boot. With quick motions, he criss-crossed the strings up her leg, tying them off at her knee. He repeated the process for her other leg.

"Alain, give me the knife," he ordered, holding out his hand. Alain grinned and handed over his prize blade. Tam draped the last scarf over the razor-sharp edge, gathered the cloth in his fist, and jerked the blade through the tough cloth. The spider silk fibers made an almost audible pop as the blade severed the wool and silk threads. Megan gasped, shocked at the destruction.

"What? So? You ladies will have to weave one extra scarf this winter. It's not like we don't have extra," Tam snorted scornfully.

"Ladies? You. You are so ... male," sputtered Megan.

He grinned at the older girl as he handed the knife back to Alain. It took less than a minute to wrap Cheobawn's forearms using half a scarf on each arm, tying them off with the leather thongs in the same manner.

"Clever," said Cheobawn, admiring her new costume.

Tam grinned at her and tousled her short blond curls. "Let's go," he said, standing up and scooping up his stick.

Cheobawn picked up her hook and whisked it around as she danced across the room, using one of the larger stick fighting styles she'd modified for her height. It was something she had invented after spying on the stick fighting classes given to the oldest boys. The cloth gaiters moved well and did not hinder her motion. The woolsey, being half spidersilk, was light and thin and would not snag on thorns or pick up burrs. She turned, immensely pleased, and caught the boys looking at her, perplexed. She froze, biting her lower lip. She had done something wrong again. They were staring at her hook.

"What?" asked Megan, "You've never seen a girl who could fight before?"

"Uh," grunted Connor, "No, I mean, yeah, it's just . . . I just never thought of the hook being a weapon until now, is all."

Alain nodded in mute agreement. Tam had a funny smile on his face, as if he'd just picked up a rock and discovered it was a bloodstone. He shook himself out of his fugue and turned towards the door without another word. Megan grinned encouragingly at Cheobawn and then turned to follow him.

Chapter Four

The east gate was just around the corner from the changing shed. Two warriors stood blocking the doors. Sixteen-year-old Sigrid seemed awkward in his leather armor. The guard position was new to him and the authority, like the leathers, did not quite sit comfortably on his shoulders. The lanky boy was dwarfed by the imposing figure of Hayrald, First Prime to the First Mother's High Coven.

Cheobawn saw the dark look on her Da's face and stopped short. It had been too good to be true, she thought, this new found freedom. Here he was, come to personally take her home, not trusting the task to anyone else.

Tam also paused, looking back at Cheobawn.

"Move it, pipsqueak," he said, grabbing her by the arm and jerking her back into motion. "You are part of my Pack now. There are rules even adults have to follow." The last was said almost as a prayer. Even Tam did not wholly trust this to be true.

When he was sure she was going to walk on her own he let her go and pushed to the head of the line, fishing in his pocket for his blue tag. He held it up in front of his face as if to ward off any evil wishes emanating from Hayrald.

"Temporary Pack, four plus one, on a foraging foray," he said nervously.

Hayrald ignored Tam. Instead he turned his gaze toward Sigrid. Sigrid flinched and stepped forward, taking the tag. With nervous fingers, he keyed in the appropriate information onto the screen set in the gatepost kiosk. Tossing the blue tag into a bin, he took a red tag from its hook on the kiosk wall. The rows and columns of tags hung neatly on their numbered hooks. Cheobawn counted the empty hooks. Twelve. Twelve groups out beyond the walls. Some would be in the fields and orchards. A few would be out beyond the well maintained fields, hunting for fresh meat while they patrolled the village perimeter. She listened to the ambient for a moment to get a general idea where they were and marked them on her mental map. The North Fork Trail was still clear for them.

Sigrid handed the red tag to Tam. That done, he stood tall and began to recite what he had obviously only just memorized.

"Tag gets you back in. Don't lose it. Gates are locked down at dusk. Do not be late. Observe and report anything of interest. Be prepared to give time, grid coordinates, and landmark references. Uh. Oh, yeah. Keep track of clicks traveled. A detailed written report along with a neatly drawn map is due on the Pack Master's desk by dawn tomorrow, no exceptions. Any contact with unfriendlies is to be reported to the guard the moment you return. No exceptions. Uh . . . " Sigrid faltered.

Cheobawn finally found the courage to look up at her Da. He was watching her intently, an odd look on his face. She waited for him to say something, anything. Instead he jerked his eyes away to pin Tam with a forbidding glare.

"There is a Black Bead in your group, Pack Leader," Mora's First Prime said. "Do you accept that burden?"

The insult cut through Cheobawn's heart like a knife. She shuddered and bit down hard on her lip to keep from making a sound. She did not need to look around to see the effect this announcement had on her new friends. The ambient flared white hot for a moment, blinding her to all else. Megan hissed in fury at her side while the boys grew silent and still.

Cheobawn blinked hard and lifted her eyes once more to look into her Da's face. He may not have been her Truefather, for what child ever knew who sired them, but he was the Father of her Heart and had been since before she could remember. Their bond went deeper than mere genetics. She silently begged for a sign of that love but he would not look at her. No smile or grimace bent her way to ease the hurt he was causing her.

Ah, she thought remotely, I knew it was too good to be true. There is always a barb hidden in the happiness of the world. It sinks into one's heart and when it gets torn out it leaves a gaping and bloody hole.

"I do accept it," Tam said loudly, his voice vibrating with the rage he could not contain.

"Do you understand that her gift is the gift of chaos? That her Luck is as unpredictable as the wind and must be guarded against?"

Bad Luck. Without saying the words, he had labeled her. Cheobawn had not thought that the world could hurt as badly as it already did, yet here was her own Da, proving her wrong. She wished with all her might that the earth might split open and swallow her down into its cool, dark belly.

The silence became complete as Hayrald waited for a response and Tam fought to contain his emotions. Cheobawn felt the ambient grow cold with his resolve.

"I will be careful with her, First Father," Tam said finally. Perhaps this was not the response Hayrald expected. A muscle quivered in the her Da's jaw. With a grunt, he turned and strode away.

The Pack stood rooted to the spot, uncertain as to what was expected next. They waited for their alpha to guide them. Tam stood frozen, staring off into the distance, a bright flush on his cheeks, seemingly unaware that the Pack stood lost and rudderless around him.

Sigrid glanced nervously after Hayrald. He looked down at the young Pack. Then he opened his mouth to say something, thought better of it, sighed, and waved them through the gate.

Tam grabbed Cheobawn by the arm in a painful grip and marched her out of the dome and down the road that cut through the fields. He did not speak as they passed the vegetable gardens, melon patches, and grain fields. He did not look down at her. He did not look around to see if the others followed. He just pounded the earth with his boots, his jaw set, his face rigid in his unexpressed fury. His anger beat at her mind like thrown stones. Cheobawn felt sick. Did he hate her? Did he regret saying yes to Megan's demands?

It was not until they passed the last of the maize fields that he stopped finally and let go of her arm. Cheobawn sank down, squatting on her heels, to bury her face in her hands. She waited there, in the darkness, for the world to stop throbbing inside her head.

"I hate him!" hissed Megan.

"Why did he do that?" growled Alain

"Who cares," Connor said. "We're out. That's all that matters."

"Yeah, but," sputtered Alain "it's like he hates her or something."

"Enough!" shouted Tam, loud enough to pull Cheobawn out of her dark reverie. "Everybody calm down. Adults are always testing you. If they get under our skin, they win. Look at us! Just a few mean words and we are all blubbering like babies." He shook his head in disgust, glaring at them. "By all that's holy, this must be a new record for a demi-Pack. Failed before we set foot outside the gate."

The Pack flinched and grew silent. They watched their leader try to get control of himself. Tam opened his mouth to shout at them again but the looks on their faces stopped him. With a groan, he spun about and stomped away, kicking at every dirt clod and stone in his path.

Cheobawn rose to her feet, guilt overwhelming her own pain. Poor Tam. She had to live with this every day. Sorrow and betrayal were old companions. For Tam, this was surely a new kind of torture. She thought about volunteering to return to the dome but she could not find the will to say those words.

The ambient still throbbed. Cheobawn turned and found Megan standing behind her, her hands curled into fists.

"Shhh," Cheobawn said, taking one of the girl's hands in her own. She caressed it until the fist relaxed. The next words that came from her lips were a prayer, words Megan had used too often to soothe Cheobawn's own hurts, words loosely borrowed from the prayers Menolly intoned amidst her smoke and ceremony on Temple Day. "Listen to the world, sister. Listen to the stars overhead. Let it go. It is nothing. A tiny thing that cannot compare to all that exists around us."

Megan frowned down at her for a moment. Then a long sigh shuddered through her body.

"How can you forgive so easily?" Megan asked softly.

"If Hayrald did not love me, it would be harder. But he does, and that makes up for most things."

Megan shook her head in disbelief. The ambient became a little less toxic.

"What hope have our men if their woman are lost?" Cheobawn said, quoting from the holy book. Megan grimaced.

"You hang around Menolly too much. You are starting to sound like a Priestess," Megan said roughly, but she wrapped her arms around Cheobawn's shoulders and pulled her close.

Cheobawn looked back at Tam.

"His heart still bleeds. We cannot go on until he is ready," Cheobawn whispered.

As if he heard her words, Tam turned his head and stared back at them. Suppressing what looked like a snarl, he returned to them, his boot heels striking the ground with firm purpose.

Megan spoke first, cutting off anything he might have said.

"You are the alpha male," she reminded him calmly, "I can go on, but I need to depend on you. I need you to stay focused. Alright?"

Tam struggled to say something to them. In desperation, he shot a pleading look at Cheobawn, as if he were about to say words that would add to the hurt already heaped upon her. Cheobawn tasted his turmoil in the ambient. She released the pain in her own heart and let the words he needed to hear fall out of her mouth.

"This is not about you. Those were Mora's words. My Da moves his lips and Mora's voice comes out," Cheobawn said. "Words meant just for me. Accept your doom, Mora wants me to hear. I cannot be like the others. I cannot pretend that I will ever be normal . . . "

Cheobawn shook her head, unable to continue. She licked her lips, tasting blood. Her finger explored the hurt and came away red. Somehow, without knowing it, she'd bitten through her lip. She touched the gory finger to her brow, anointing her skin with the macabre war paint, the pattern much like those that Menolly painted on the faces of the penitents in the Blood Rites on Darkday.

"I can go back," she sighed in resignation. "You have the map. You do not need me."

Tam brushed her hands away from her face, his own face gone soft, his mind full of resolve that bled through the ambient and eased all the hurt in her heart.

"Squeaker's twaddle," he said, pouring a bit of water from his water skin into the palm of his hand and washing her face and hands with it. "I know what I know. They are wrong. Forget them. Fate has brought us together. The only real thing is our Pack. Nothing else matters. If we stand united against them, they cannot destroy us."

Cheobawn stared at him, surprised by his certainty. Tam's passion was premature at best. They had only just Packed and already this Alpha male had them bound and wed. What did this deeply complicated boy know that she did not?

Tam pulled a medstick from one of his many pockets. They were used to stop the bleeding of the minor scuffs received in sparring and Cheobawn wondered that he had one handy. Not all the demi-Pack's battles for rank took place in the safety of the practice rooms. This thought hinted at dark burdens and hidden depths under Tam's perfect exterior. As he dabbed the astringent end on her wounded lip, she wondered if she and he had more in common than she first thought.

"No more bleeding," he scolded her sternly. "It attracts all sorts of nasties."

Cheobawn looked up into his eyes, admiring his stubborn

determination. Were they Pack and not just a temporary thing? She knew he was wrong but for him she would make herself believe his hopeful words. If she pretended they were true then maybe they would become true. Wrapping the fantasy of her own Pack around her like a warm coat, she smiled.

"That's what I want to see!" he said encouragingly, smiling back. He looked up into the worried eyes of the rest of his teammates. "I will take point with Cheobawn. Connor next, then Megan. Al, you take rear guard. Keep a stick's length apart, no less, no more. Let's practice our Battle Trail maneuvers. No talking. Come on, everybody. We are going to have some fun!"

Taking Cheobawn by the hand, he turned and strode down the East Trail, his troop close behind.

Chapter Five

Tam's pace was measured, his strides wide. His legs ate the distance effortlessly. Cheobawn reviewed what she knew about Battle Trail. It was a more complicated form of Dancing Molly—follow the leader, doing what they do, stepping where they step. Add complete silence and you got Battle Trail. You could still talk but you had to do it using fingersign and forest sounds. She knew fingersign better than most girls her age. Da had been teaching her since before she could remember. It was something they did to pass the time while waiting for Mora and the Coven to stop being busy and notice them.

They left the cultivated fields and orchards behind and entered the forest. The trees blocked the sky and closed in behind them, casting a perpetual twilight on the forest floor.

As Cheobawn's eyes became accustomed to the gloom, details revealed themselves. Birds and insects and treehoppers of every kind buzzed and chittered softly in the canopy high above their heads. Croakers called from their hiding places under the ferns and squeakers sang from the miniature pools inside watercups clinging like great green insects to the tree trunks. Cheobawn tried to see everything, thrilled at each new sight. This was so much better than the photos and videos she studied in class.

It was hard to see everything she wanted to see and still keep up with Tam. Cheobawn, being more than a head shorter than her leader, managed to match his pace but she had to take three steps for his two. It took all her concentration and most of her energy. She did not protest. Tam's plan called for speed. She did not want to be the one to slow them down. But more importantly, she did not want Tam to regret his decision to let her join them. This was her problem. She would solve it.

She listened to her body. She listened to the ambient. She watched Tam's rhythms and there she found a solution. She let her body feel his as if it were her own, matching his heartbeat and breathing. She set her legs to mimic his every step, pushing her stride wider, letting him pick the best places on the trail to put their feet. After that it was just a matter of getting out of the way and letting the process of walking take over. She smiled, pleased at her own ingenuity. Turning her attention back to the scenery, she reveled in the feeling of being truly free in a place of profound beauty for the very first time in her life.

She listened to the trees. Each one seemed different from the next, like a single voice in a choir. One could focus on a solitary tree but the true beauty came in their harmonies. Together they were one organism draped like a living skin on the land from the edge of the snowfields high on the mountains all the way down to the infinite cliffs of the Escarpment to the south.

Cheobawn wanted to hold her breath so she could hear the trees talking to each other but her laboring heart brought her out of her reverie. Borrowing rhythm and pattern from Tam was one thing. Borrowing energy was another problem. By the time they reached the fork in the road and turned up the lesser traveled North Fork Trail, the strain of trying to match Tam's bigger strides was turning her legs to jelly. As the trail rose before her, she struggled for a moment, determined to keep up. It was becoming a point of personal pride that she not be the first to break under the relentless pace.

Merely sucking more air into her lungs was not enough. She needed more than air. She listened to the forest around her. Life infused everything, filling the ambient with energy that hung in a heavy cloud just off the edge of seeing. She drew it in like air, breathing it into her heart and her legs and her lungs, filling herself up with it, using what she needed before letting the excess run back into the ground through her boot heels. The pain and fatigue disappeared immediately. It took no more than a dozen steps to set the rhythm of this energy flow in her head. She had no difficulty matching Tam step for step with this borrowed vigor after that.

The more she listened to the forest the more it became solid and real in her mind. Everything glowed. Trotting on, she watched this overlay of light as it played out around the trees and the ferns. Buzzers left trails of light in their wake. She could tell where the hoppers hid in their burrows by the bright spots they made in the ambient above their dens.

She grinned in delight. It did not take much of a leap of imagination to pretend that the stones of the mountain under her feet were the bones of some monstrously huge bear and that all the living things in the forest were part of its living pelt.

Cheobawn thought about what it must be like to be this bear. Did the fall of her boots upon stone tickle his furry sides? She dance behind Tam, daring it to wake.

With her mind full, she ran blind, trusting Tam to guide her feet, her connection to his mind her lifeline, while her eyes flitted from one amazing sight to the next. Sunlight broke through the dense canopy in random places, making columns of golden light in the humid air. Flutterflies and gnats and buzzing nasties danced through the light like falling stars. The blooms of the parasitic sugarsips hanging off the lowest branches, garish in their yellow and pink displays, were the only thing to relieve the constant theme of greenery. A bit of sweet nectar lay at the base of each flower. Cheobawn eyed them longingly. Perhaps on the way back, she could sample their liquor.

She did not see the large root that Tam jumped over until almost too late. She got over it, but only just, her heel skidding down the opposite side, making her lurch and stumble. Somehow Tam sensed it. He spun on one toe and shot out a hand, catching her outstretched arm, keeping her on her feet.

He held up his fist, and the Pack, alert to his signals, stopped.

Alright? Tam fingersigned while his eyes sized up her condition.

Trying not to breath hard, Cheobawn nodded stoically then thought better of it. Drink? she asked. Even here, in the shade, the heat of high summer found them and turned the damp rising from the dead leaves into steam. Tam nodded and signaled the same to the others.

Cheobawn pulled her waterskin off her belt and took a long drink. Tam touched her hand.

Slow. A little bit. Too much gets you sick, he signed. She nodded.

A sound, deep and ominous, like the groan of a giant, filtered through the canopy above her head. Cheobawn jumped, her head still full of giant sleeping bears. She looked around, wide eyed, trying to sense the danger in the ambient as her heart pounded in her chest. No one else seemed to be alarmed, not the birds, or the treehoppers or the croakers or the buzzy bugs. Not even her Pack.

Tam touched her shoulder to get her attention. *Trees,* his fingers said. She frowned and made the query sign.

Watch me, he signed. He pointed the fingers of both hands at the sky and waved his arms back and forth, blowing on them. Trees in the wind. She frowned, not quite understanding how that would make such a noise. Tam blew harder and his tree hands bent against each other, the fingers locking and rubbing together. She cocked her head, puzzled. *Living wood,* he signed. Then he rubbed his two index fingers together.

The sound came again and suddenly it made sense. She stared up at the canopy, enchanted. The trees had voices, only they needed a neighbor to help them speak. Trees, it seemed, needed friends as much as humans. Tam touched her shoulder again.

Understand? his fingers asked.

Cheobawn nodded happily. *Tree Packs make tree songs,* she signed.

Tam opened his mouth to laugh but stopped himself. Connor snorted. Tam snapped a *quiet* sign at him. Cheobawn glanced back at the others, smiling.

Connor's fingers flashed the symbols for *new cub just opening eyes.*

Cheobawn stuck her tongue out at him, returning with *fenelk hindquarter.*

Megan scowled fiercely at her.

Stop! the older girl signed, in no uncertain terms. Cheobawn reconsidered the fun of starting a sign argument with Connor and turned around to find Tam with his arms folded, tapping his fingers for effect.

Cheobawn smiled up at him innocently.

Ready? he queried with a stern look. He did not wait for a reply. With a shake of his head, he turned and continued jogging up the trail, but at a slightly slower pace, shortening his stride so Cheobawn did not have to work so hard to keep up.

The trees thinned as they climbed, needletrees replacing the cedars and blackoaks. The thick blanket of dead leaves thinned to let grasses and sedges grow in the sunny places between stands of longpines. A golden furred treehopper scolded them from the safety of its perch, high above their heads. Tam stopped to point out tracks that crossed the trail heading up-slope. Sharp three-toed hooves had left deep marks in the soft clay. *Grunter,* Tam signed, touching a print. Overlaid atop the grunter's prints was the mark of a large cat. The paw prints were twice the size of her hand and crossed the trail, heading up the mountain in the same direction as the herd of tusked grazers. Cheobawn scanned the branches overhead, fearful of an ambush, but Tam tugged at her ear to catch her attention.

Old spoor. Edges crumbling. More than a day. Long gone. We are safe, he signed with a smile. She checked the ambient. Nothing hunted them there. She grinned sheepishly at Tam, feeling foolish. She had forgotten, for a moment, that she was anything but an ordinary girl taking a stroll in a strange forest and that part of her job as Ear was to keep watch in the ambient. Tam returned her smile and then turned and led them on.

Somewhere well past the two click mark on the map in Cheobawn's head, the trail curved upwards to follow the edge of a ravine that cut deeply into the side of the mountain. Tam paused and pulled out the map to check their location. Satisfied, he stepped off the path and jogged down a ridge line, taking care where he placed his feet on this unfamiliar and uneven ground. She noted his care and mimicked it. The mountain had no patience for the careless and the unwary, all the teachers said. Carelessness led to injury. Injury, this far from the dome, could become almost certain death.

It took a few strides to adjust her pace to the soft earth littered with stones and low growing sedges that wanted to catch at an unwary foot. Tam paused and glanced back. She grinned at him. He returned her smiled, obviously pleased that he did not have to remind her to take care.

Not long after, a fernhen clucked in annoyance and fluttered, broken-winged, into a thicket. Cheobawn stopped to watch the mother fowl's ruse. This was the same ploy used by the little pipers who nested under the melon leaves around Home Dome. Somewhere, probably very nearly under their feet, a nest full of eggs lay hidden. Cheobawn marked the place in her head for their return trip. Fernhen eggs were a precious delicacy. The Mothers on kitchen duty would be pleased.

At the bottom of the slope, a wall of tubegrass stopped them. This was not the tame stuff grown in the hedgerows inside the dome. The wild stands grew as high as four grown men and became so densely packed that one would be hard pressed to squeeze a hand through the stalks. Tam pulled out his map again, perhaps trying to find the best way around it. The rest of the Pack stopped and sipped from their waterskins.

They were very nearly there. Cheobawn could feel it. The happy bubbly feeling beckoned her onward. It was close. Very close. She felt more than heard the sound of trickling water coming from somewhere inside the dense copse. They needed to get inside the stand of tubegrass.

She touched the back of Tam's hand and motioned him to follow. He raised his brows but then shrugged and motioned her on.

Chapter Six

Cheobawn let the feelings in the ambient lead her off to the right and a little downhill. She did not check to see if anyone followed but was reassured by the sound of footfalls behind her. The feelings in the ambient drew her on.

The stand of grass was immense, at least a quarter of the size of the village dome. Half way around it she found what she was looking for. A tiny brook fought free of the thirsty tubegrass, trickling around a barricade of boulders and stalks in a dozen places before rejoining in a deep pool before continuing its journey down the mountain. The tubegrass roots could find no good purchase among the large stones, creating a tunnel through the tangle. Cheobawn stepped into the water and followed the flow uphill.

It was not an easy path. She found herself clinging to the overhanging foliage to steady herself as she navigated her way over slippery stones and around moss-covered boulders. The undergrowth closed in over their heads, shutting out the sound of the forest beyond. The labored breathing of the children filled that silence.

Cheobawn was small but even she had trouble in spots. She pulled her hooked stick off her belt and hacked at the small stalks that blocked her way. The bigger children had a harder time of it. The sound of their bladed sticks rang as they enlarged the tunnel through which they crawled.

Eventually, the stream, along with all the rocks and boulders, disappeared under a deep blanket of gravel deposited by some ancient flood. Nothing but moss grew on this unstable ground. Cheobawn paused to stare in wonder at the protected glade that had formed inside the depths of the wild grass. She rose from her stooped crawl and stepped out into the open, smiling up at the blue sky overhead.

The ambient beckoned. She went exploring. The tubegrass would not grow in the gravel but other things flourished in the wet ground. A stand of gorgeberry bushes, laden with fruit, grew between the walls of grass. There were so many ripe berries, the smell saturated the air with their sweet perfume.

Cheobawn approached the closest bush cautiously. It seemed to be unnaturally animated. As she drew near, she could see why. Buzzy things of every description hovered in a thick cloud around the large bushes. Some skipped from berry to berry lapping up the sweet juice that oozed from bruised and crushed fruit, jousting for room at the best spots. Others clung to the leaves and twigs, exhausted from their feasting. Dozens of groggy birds—chikchiks, gnat catchers, blackbirds and more that Cheobawn did not recognize—roosted on the branches, heads tucked under their wings. Some, too exhausted to even cling to a branch, littered the moss under the trees. They flapped feebly and waddled away slowly as Cheobawn approached, chittering grumpily at being forced to move. She laughed, for it reminded her of the complaints of the oldmas reluctant to move out of their chairs when the evening bells rang reminding them that it was time to move to their beds.

Cheobawn picked her way carefully around the fat birds to the nearest bush and plucked a golden berry from a branch just before a small chikchik could claim it. The bird scolded her in half-hearted annoyance but Cheobawn ignored it, popping the berry into her mouth. Its flavor burst out onto her tongue, warm and sweet with just a small bite of bitter. She chewed slowly, trying to remember every nuance of the moment, then swallowed and smiled. There was a delightful fuzzy aftertaste that she did not remember from the gorgeberries she had eaten at home. Perhaps things always tasted better, plucked fresh off the tree.

She was tempted to stuff her mouth but starting the fun without the remainder of her Pack seemed rude. While she waited she gathered moss, lining her basket with it, to make a soft nest for the fernhen eggs she meant to collect on the return home.

By the time the rest of the children emerged from the green tunnel, wet, tired, and highly annoyed, she had shed her pack, boots, and gaiters and was digging her bare toes deep into the carpet of damp moss while nibbling on a handful of berries. Megan straightened with a groan, looking cross, her curls plastered to her sweaty face. Cheobawn grinned at her Pack and held out her hand.

"Hurry, before the birds get them all," she said out loud, foregoing fingersign.

"Shhh," hissed Megan.

"Don't worry. The grass keeps the sound inside," Cheobawn said. "We can relax and have fun."

Alain and Connor did not need a second invitation. They shed their sticks and their gleaning baskets, dropping them as they ran towards the nearest bush. A small cloud of insects rose lazily from under their feet. Alain won the race, elbowing Connor aside with a growl. The smallest boy, resigned to being the low man in the hierarchy of his demi-Pack, switched direction mid stride and headed for the next bush. There were many bushes and many berries. Far too many for a trio of ravenous small boys to devour in one sitting. The contest for position could be postponed for one more day.

Tam and Megan, taking their rank seriously, followed more sedately, perhaps being more reluctant to be weaponless. Tam scowled after the boys as they wandered off into the grove, a worried look on his face.

"We are safe here," Cheobawn reassured him, chewing on a berry. "Nothing big can get in past the tubegrass. Ask Megan."

Megan shrugged.

"We are in a gray area," she said.

"Huh?" The look on his face said something of his dislike of surprises.

"From the moment we deviated from the official foray plan, the ambient went gray. That means we are in a bit of danger, but only from the adults back at Home Dome. We are in trouble, but we knew that the minute we handed in our foray form."

"But are we safe here?" Tam asked again.

"Hmm, depends," the older girl said as she plucked a berry and placed it delicately in her mouth. She closed her eyes and sighed. Tam watched her, waiting. Megan opened her eyes to find Tam still waiting for an answer. She held out a berry.

"It depends on whether we are caught or not. It depends on how bad we are going to be punished when we get home. Try this. It's just a gorgeberry. What could it hurt?" she asked him. Tam took it, making a visible effort to relax.

"Wow," Tam said, chewing. "I don't remember a berry ever tasting this good."

"I know," Megan agreed, popping a few more in her mouth.

"We should fill our baskets for everyone in the dome," Tam said, dropping his basket off his shoulders and walking away as he shoved a handful of fruit into his mouth.

"We should," agreed Megan, pulling a spray of berries off a branch. She wandered away, nibbling on them as she looked about the glen with wonder.

Tam picked up one of the engorged birds and put it on a branch. It fluffed its feathers and immediately went back to sleep. Megan picked up a jewel-winged flutterfly and placed it in her hair. Tam laughed and did the same with a beetle, its carapace flashing iridescent blue in the bright sunlight. Cheobawn followed the two alpha leaders and mimicked their play. She gingerly picked up a scarlet flutterfly and when it did not move to defend itself, she hung it from her ear and giggled when its little feet tickled. She adorned her other ear in kind and added a trio to the top of her head to create a brilliant crown.

The Pack wandered through the grove, eating as they went, adorning the trees and themselves with stuporous wildlife. It became an endlessly amusing game. Alain and Connor disappeared in the direction of the sound of running water, chasing each other from bush to bush looking for the most perfect berry. Alain invariably won.

"This is so great, Cheobawn," Tam sighed from around his tenth mouthful of berries. "I'll let you take me out for fun anytime you want."

Cheobawn opened her mouth to say thank you but then it occurred to her that the berries and the birds and the bugs were not the best part of her fun spot. Something was about to happen. She snapped off a handful of berry laden branches and began passing them out to the two Alphas, ignoring any question or protest. When everyone had a branch in each hand, she positioned them in just the right spots. Then she went to stand on her own patch of moss.

Cheobawn looked down at her feet, shifted them to what seemed the right place, and then held the branches out, trying to convince the ambient that she was a gorgeberry bush.

"What ever are we doing, Ch'che?" asked Megan.

"The berries are not the fun. The berries bring the fun. Do what I do."

"What are we doing?" Tam asked Megan.

"I have no idea. Best to play along," said Megan from around a mouthful of berries.

"Be a bush," hissed Cheobawn. "Hurry, before it is too late."

Megan looked at Tam and shrugged. She held out her branches.

"Megan, move your left foot over about a hands width," instructed Cheobawn, listening to the place at Megan's feet. Megan complied.

Tam, smiling indulgently, raised his arms into the air.

"Tam. Closer to the water. There. Now move your right foot a bit. Perfect," Cheobawn instructed. Connor and Alain wandered back, berry stained and smiling.

"Whatcha doing?" Alain asked.

"Waiting," Cheobawn whispered.

"For what?" Connor whispered back.

"For that," said Cheobawn, pointing at the moss at her feet with her chin.

The moss was moving.

"By the Goddess!" Alain screeched, dancing off the moss to

stand on the tip of a rock poking through gravel. Connor joined him. They clung to each other, wide-eyed and confused.

"Don't move," Cheobawn yelled sternly. "You will crush them. Hold still. They will climb in search of fruit."

"Wee bit," Tam said through clenched teeth, trying to sound calm. "What, exactly, is under the moss?"

"No idea," Cheobawn said with a shrug. "Something fun," she added encouragingly.

Tam closed his eyes and shook his head, looking grim but patient. Megan watched the heaving moss and then looked back at her small friend, an uncertain frown on her face.

"What do you mean, you don't know?" she asked.

"I don't know their name. Laid as eggs before the first frost. Slept the winter through. Grow as the heat of the summer grows. Now they are being born. The heat awakens the sleepers and ripens the berries at the same time. They will climb to find food and then fly away."

Megan looked over at Tam.

"Do you know what kind of bug does that?"

Tam shook his head, distracted by the sight of the moss breaking open at his feet. A pointed head with scissor-like jaws pushed its way clear and looked around with small, crimson eyes. Not an insect. A lizard.

"Oh, my . . . " breathed Megan. As if by unspoken signal, hundreds of heads now emerged.

"Don't. Move," hissed Cheobawn. A lizard by Tam's foot struggled for a moment and then shook its way free of the moss. Its body was as long as her hand, its milky skin almost transparent. If they held still you could almost see their hearts beating inside their chests.

"Glasslizards," breathed Megan in wonder.

In a flash, the lizard was up Tam's leg, pausing to cling to his belt. As if this was an unspoken signal, a thousand more reptiles struggled free and made the mad dash to the nearest thing that resembled a tree. That included five small children who were doing their best to behave tree-like without yelping in delight. Soon they all had at least three perched on the tops of their heads and another dozen jostling for space on each arm. The branches of the trees around them drooped under the weight of lizard flesh.

Cheobawn began to giggle. Tiny lizard toes tickled her skin and the grumpy look they gave her when they found no berries hanging from her nose delighted her. A small brawl was taking place around the berries on the branches in her hands. Megan yipped in pain and dropped one of her branches, shaking her hand. The displaced lizards, robbed of their perch, leapt into the air. The movement startled those around the tall girl and as if by consensus, all the lizards in the grove launched themselves into the air and spread their limbs wide.

Cheobawn gasped in awe. This was why they were called glasslizards. A membrane as clear as glass, held taught between the front and back legs, spread wide to catch the air. They were gliders. She tilted her head up and threw her arms wide as she watched the pale blizzard of wings and tails fill the the brilliant blue sky. Her heart was so full of happiness it hurt to contain it. Unable to stop herself, she filled the ambient with her pleasure, laughing. Whether it was the sound of her delight or the bliss in her mind, the boys joined in.

Cheobawn looked over at Megan and caught the older girl staring at her, her face gone soft, her eyes wide, caught up in the little girl's pleasure. Cheobawn cocked her head and raised an eyebrow, sending her friend a silent apology. A smile twitched at the corners of Megan's mouth as if to tell her all was forgiven for this breach of manners.

Looking down, Cheobawn found a straggler still clinging to her shirt. She carefully plucked it off and held it captive in the palm of her hand to study it closely. The little heart fluttered inside its chest, sending blood coursing through all the tiny veins in its body. Muscles and bones moved under the skin, like an animated anatomy video. She tossed it into the air to watch it glide away then chased after others, catching them to hand feed them berries just for the pleasure of watching the berries slide down transparent throats.

When both children and lizards seemed to have had their fill of fun, the lizards leapt into the air and soared away into the blades of tubegrass.

"Oooh," mewed Megan sadly, watching the last of the glasslizards leave from where she lay on the moss, the sun warming her upturned face, "Where are they going?"

"I remember reading that their summer range is in the high meadows," Tam said, trying to keep his pet lizard captive for one more moment. The lizard could not be persuaded to stay, ignoring his proffered berry. Soon, Tam let it go. It leapt away, the sun flashing on the membranes of its wings. He sighed, happy and content, and lay back on the soft moss.

Alain nodded, heavy-eyed, in the shade of a gorgeberry bush.

"Do you think we can come back here when they return to lay their eggs?" Megan asked sleepily.

"That would be fun," Tam said, nibbling lazily on the last of his berries.

Cheobawn did not want to waste a moment in sleep. She heard Connor whooping in delight further up the glen. The grove held more fun than just berries and lizards, it seemed.

Leaving the others to rest in the heat of the midday, she ran towards the sound. At the far end of the grove a tumble of boulders hid a series of pools connected by miniature waterfalls. She found him waist-deep in the largest pool. He was rapidly ridding himself of all his soaked clothing and tossing it up on the bank.

Cheobawn laughed, feeling giddy and light-headed with happiness.

"No, no, you have it all backwards," she yelled. "You take a bath after you get undressed, not before."

"Come in. It's perfect!" shouted Connor.

Cheobawn shed her clothes, leaving them on a flat rock high above the wet and jumped into the water, naked except for her omeh.

Connor had lied. Having only just emerged from the bowels of the mountain, the water was shockingly cold after the heat of the sunny summer afternoon. She rose to the surface and let out a strangled screech. Connor grinned at her, his teeth chattering. She splashed water in his direction as payment for tricking her. An all-out war ensued to see who could douse the other more. When they could no longer feel their fingers and Connors lips had taken on an alarming shade of blue, they called a truce and hauled themselves out to dry, bellies pressed flat onto the heat of the nearby boulders. Cheobawn hugged the stone, letting it bake her while she listened absently to the ambient. The midday air hung heavy over the grove as the lizards buzzed softly somewhere out in the tall grass and the birds in the gorgeberry bushes chirped at each other, too lazy to even sing their songs properly.

Cheobawn opened one sleepy eye and found Connor's eyes fixed on her omeh, a slightly befuddled look on his face.

"Can I ask you something?" Connor said, propping his chin on his fist, as if holding his head up was very hard work.

"Sure," Cheobawn said. Here it comes, she thought, the questions she could not answer.

"You are the best Ear ever. How did you manage to . . . ya know?"

"How did I mess up my Choosingday?"

"Yeah," Connor said, the look on his face one of honest puzzlement. "You can see across five clicks of forest and find a swarm of glasslizards on hatching day. How could you not see into two stupid boxes? No offense intended but the Choosingday psi test is so easy even half the boys can pass it."

Perhaps the sunshine and laughter had softened the walls around her heart. Perhaps it was because Connor had played with her with child-like abandon, as no other child of the domes ever had. Perhaps it was the way he asked, without judgment or revulsion. Perhaps she owed her Pack an explanation. Perhaps friends were supposed to share their most intimate secrets, secrets never ever shared with another living soul.

"I hate dolls," Cheobawn said simply. This was not the whole truth, being only the first layer of a very complicated secret, but it was a start.

"Huh? What do dolls have to do with taking a dead simple test? Pick the good, leave the bad. How hard is that?"

"I wanted a pet, but Mora always gave me dolls, instead. I was mad at her that day and they did not know that I could see into the boxes."

Connor began to giggle.

"They gave you a choice between a doll and . . . what? Acid Scorpions?"

"A fuzzy," she corrected.

"No! Really?" he laughed, "Don't tell me that given a choice between a doll and a vicious little fur-ball with teeth, you chose the fur-ball?"

"I was three," Cheobawn growled at him, turning her face away and pretending to sleep. Connor was trying not to laugh, but was not doing a very good job of it. She could hear muffled hiccups coming out from around the fist he must have buried in his mouth.

Cheobawn turned over and stared up at the deep blue sky.

"I wasn't going to open the box," she lied, pasting a grumpy look on her face.

"No," sighed Connor in a strangled voice. "I should hope not."

Cheobawn let a small smile play across the corners of her mouth as she let herself remember that day for the first time in a very long while. Choosingday was the test when Amabel. The domes resident Maker of the Living Thread, found out if the thing she had created inside her labs had been bred true. A feast day, full of celebration, that hid a brutal heart. A test Cheobawn had failed miserably, winning the dubious honor of wearing a black bead in her omeh for the rest of her life.

Bits and pieces of the ceremony still clung tenaciously to the dark corners of her mind. She remembered Hayrald clearly. He had been the rock she had clung to. Like a stone wall, he had been there, standing between her and the knives of the Coven. She remembered Mora. Mora had been furious.

"You should have been there. The look on Mora's face . . ."

Connor rolled over and fell off his rock, howling with laughter. Cheobawn scowled at him. It had not been funny. But now, in retrospect, from Connor's point of view, it bordered on ludicrous. His laughter became infectious. She joined in, laughing until her sides hurt and she had to beg Connor to stop more than once. At last, Connor wiped his eyes and lay back on his rock, sighing with contentment.

"You are one weird little kid, did you know that?" Connor said sleepily from behind closed eyelids. "I am glad we are Pack-mates."

Cheobawn turned her head and stared at his relaxed profile. What did one say to a person who had just taken a lead weight off her heart and set her free?

"Thank you," she said softly.

Chapter Seven

Cheobawn woke with a start and stared up at the sky, her heart thumping madly in her chest. Something was wrong. Something in the ambient desperately needed her attention.

She felt funny. A fuzzy taste coated her tongue and a dull headache hung at the back of her skull. Was she catching a cold? She lifted her head. Pain lanced through her brain and set off skyrockets behind her eyes. She groaned and rolled off the rock, holding her temples to keep them from exploding. Sucking in great gulps of air to force down the rising nausea, she dug the fingers of her perception deep into the energy of the mountain, drawing it into herself. The world wobbled and tried to right itself. It was hard. Harder than it should have been. The shards of light flickering behind her closed eyes made it hard to think. She stole from the flesh of the world to burn away her illness and when she thought she could do it without throwing up, she stood and looked around.

Connor snored loudly from the next rock. She kicked him in the hip with her big toe.

"Wake up."

Connor snorted but did not wake. Instead, he rolled over and continued sleeping.

This was all wrong, so very wrong. She was getting really, really scared. The mountain's ambient fluttered inside her chest like a candle guttering in a strong wind. She closed her eyes and tasted things one by one. She tasted the spring, then the moss and the trees and the lizards. Her imagination filled in the gaps of her understanding. She was suddenly filled with an absolute certainty that they had overstayed their welcome upon the side of the great mountain bear and that the monster was about to shake them all off.

Terror filled her. She lifted her face to the sky and opened her eyes wide to see what the mountain wanted to tell her. She moaned as she realized what was wrong.

While they had been sleeping the sun had fallen out of zenith and was now nearly touching the tops of the tubegrass. Late! Night was coming and they were hours from Home Dome.

She grabbed Connor's shoulder and shook him roughly. His head rolled drunkenly to the side as his eyes opened a crack and tried to focus on her.

"Get up! It's time to go," she yelled.

"Huh? What are you going on about?" Connor asked groggily. She grabbed his arm and rolled him off the rock into the soggy moss.

"Hey!" he yelled, getting annoyed. Annoyance was not enough, she realized. She needed him angry. She slapped him. Connor roared and sent a fist flying at her head. She dodged it, but just barely, leaping away when he tried to come after her.

"We slept too long!" she shouted at him, "Get dressed! Fast!"

Connor stared in horror at the pale sky.

"Where are the others? Why did they let us sleep so long?" he asked, fury warring with terror.

Cheobawn looked downstream, suddenly wondering the same thing. She pulled on her tunic and shorts, shoved her feet into her boot liners, slipped them into her boots without lacing them up and then scooped up her hook. She looked over at Connor. He had on his damp pants and shirt but he was struggling with his soggy boots.

"No time. Tie them later," she hissed, gathering up what she could find of his equipment and shoving it into his hands. She pulled him to his feet and handed him his bladed stick. When she was sure he would follow her, she turned and raced through the trees, hunting for the rest of her friends.

Tam sat hunched over, his head in his hands. Alain was busy throwing up behind a boulder. Megan, thank the goddess, was on her feet, albeit looking a little unsteady. She was staring in horror at the sky, whimpering.

Cheobawn grabbed the older girl by the hand but Megan jerked away, a look of utter panic on her face. Cheobawn knew what lay behind that look. Megan was listening to her Luck and finding only darkness.

"We have to leave! You have to get us home," Cheobawn said urgently, grabbing the older girl's arms and shaking them roughly.

"There is no place to go. Do you feel it? The world has turned into ice. We are dead," Megan whispered in panic. She spun around, a look of madness in her eyes as if she was trying to see through the walls of the grove.

Cheobawn wanted to weep in despair, but it was a luxury she could not afford. In the ambient, the great monster, Bear Under the Mountain, chased the clouds across her sky mind. Be fierce, little hopper, it whispered. Fierce was not kind, she thought back at her imaginary companion, nor was it nice. Amused, the mountain bear agreed. Blocking Megan's feelings from her heart, she abandoned her friend and went looking for someone who would save them.

Tam was on his feet, now, but looking gray faced. She crossed to him and punched him in the thigh.

"Ow! What was that for?"

"Stick your fingers down your throat, if it will help," Cheobawn growled without pity, "I need you to hear me. The mountain is in motion. The night hunters will move down the slopes at dusk and we cannot be outside when this happens."

"I feel like I have been at the oldpa's beer keg," Tam groaned, leaning over. Cheobawn skipped out of the way as his stomach contents spattered over the moss. He straightened up, wiping his mouth, his eyes staring suspiciously from the disgusting heap of berry mash at his feet to the bushes around them. "Oh, by the Goddess, we got drunk on berries. Why did you not stop me? What kind of Ear lets her Pack get all messed up?"

Cheobawn punched him again, in the other thigh, furious that he could not hear what she was trying to say.

"The lizards were the gift, not the berries," Cheobawn said defensively. "We have no time. We have to go. Now!"

"Give me a minute. My head is spinning."

"Listen!" she shouted, stamping her feet in frustration. "We are out of time!"

Tam turned, looking for something. He nearly fell but managed to save himself.

"Have you seen my blade? I need my blade."

She thought better of hitting him again. He was in far worse shape than Connor. Looking around frantically for anyone or anything that might help her get them on their feet and out of this grove, she spotted Alain. He had collapsed to his knees, his vomiting having turned into continuous dry heaves. She turned to check on Megan. Overwhelmed, the older girl now crouched down with her face pressed against her knees.

Nothing in this grove would save them, it was certain. She cast her mind out into the forest beyond, seeking help. The Bear Under the Mountain laughed at her request for aid. *Only the strong survive,* it whispered to her, *all else is eaten. Time is not your friend. Run, little hopper, run!*

Despair knocked at the door of her heart again but she snarled fiercely at it and refused it entrance.

She was an Ear. What was an Ear supposed to do?

Cheobawn checked the ambient for traces of her future self. The future was in chaos.

Her brain scrambled to find a future timeline in which they all survived. She caught up the multiple threads of the Pack's future, plucking them one by one. Options that included them living to see the end of the day were slipping rapidly through her fingers like sand. She stared at Tam. He was the key. She tried to see into his head and decipher what it would take to get him moving.

He was Alpha and male. This was his Pack. This was his first foray. He would argue with everything but what had been drilled into him as being right and dutiful. Arguing would waste time and wasting time would kill them.

She turned and ran through the grove, picking up weapons and packs and water skins. She returned, staggering under the load and handed them out.

"Hurry," she said over and over again.

Alain struggled with the straps of his pack, his movements broken and uncoordinated.

Tam took his water skin and drank deeply, nearly draining it. Cheobawn wanted to scream in frustration at their unnecessary delays but she resisted the urge. Instead she helped Megan don her pack. She ran from Tam, to Alain, to Megan, shoving arms through shoulder straps, securing buckles, tightening laces and pressing weapons into loose fingered hands. She took pity on Alain, the sickest of them and tried to lighten his load. She took his water skin and gave it to Tam, then took the hunting knife from his belt and put it on her own.

Just when she thought she might get them all moving in the right direction, Connor stumbled into the clearing, barely dressed, one boot on, the other still in his hand, looking as scared as she felt.

Connor. She had forgotten Connor. The error shocked her to her core and left her shaking. She stopped and tried to calm the panic that was eating her mind. If she could forget one of her own, what else had she left undone? What else had she overlooked?

It was then that she noticed her badly secured boots. Too much, her mind whispered. You have forgotten everything that will keep you alive. It was no use rushing out, unprepared. The mountain would just kill them that much quicker. She stooped and laced up her boots properly, tying them snug to keep them from rubbing. Then she hunted down her own pack where she had left it on the edge of the grove. Opening it, she pulled her leggings from its depths. She re-wrapped her calves and forearms just as Tam had done for her that morning, taking great care with cloth and laces. Snag bare skin on a thorn and the smell of blood would draw in the predators. It was the small things like this that killed people, the teaching stories said.

Terror washed over her. Not all of it was her own. She recited the mantra against fear, wishing calm upon the ambient.

"What is fear?" she breathed. "Fear is nothing. Fear is illusion. Pass through its fire. Truth lies at its core. What is truth?" She stood up, feeling calmer and glared up at the sinking sun. "I am Truth," she whispered fiercely.

She checked the ambient of the mountain once more, breathing it in, letting it fill her before releasing it back to its place in the world. Things were not getting any better out there, beyond the limits of the grove but they still had a chance.

She tried to think of a complete course of action but she could not see her way clear to the end. Too much uncertainty lay between this moment and the act of walking up to the gate and handing over their red tag. There were things out there that she could not control. Too many threads wanted to unravel. Too many obstacles needed to be overcome. Each plan fell apart in her mind long before the end.

But there were certainties. Places that beckoned like lights in the dark. Goals. Reach one at the right time and the next one became possible. Their path would not be a straight line from here to there but a zigzag trail that might add another click in distance to a journey that was already too far for five sick children with very little time left to them. If she thought they could survive the night in this grove she would stay and try going home in the morning but the grove shivered in the ambient with catastrophic changes.

She found her Pack standing where she had left them, angry looks on their faces, color bright in their cheeks. They had been arguing. Connor had his boots on, at least.

She slid her pack off one arm and opened it, pulling out a ration tin. She squatted down on the moss between Tam and Connor and looked over at Alain and Megan. Their circle was complete.

Breaking the seal on the tin, Cheobawn removed the lid and examined the contents. She took her time picking out the right morsel, but eventually she popped a nutpaste bit into her mouth and chewed it slowly, taking a moment to appreciate its sweet saltiness. She looked up. All eyes were on her. Good. She had their attention. Without thinking, she let the words fall out of her mouth as needed.

"We have not eaten anything but berries since breakfast and here it is, nearly supper time," she said calmly. "Eat something. Not much. We must run home and you will not run well on a full stomach. Put some of the bits in your pockets to eat as you run."

She waited, holding her breath. Connor squatted, hesitantly following her lead. Alain and Megan did not need any more of an invitation to sit, both still wobbly on their feet. Tam was the last. Cheobawn did not have to look into his face to know he was angry. The emotion bled off him like a wind, whipping around her, eroding her calm.

"We have a problem. More than a few, to be truthful," Cheobawn said evenly, nibbling on a piece of smoked dried meat. She looked into Megan's face. The older girl's eyes were two dark holes in a pale and frozen mask. It was taking everything in their Alpha Ear's power to maintain control. "Megan knows. The ambient is telling her things. She knows that we will die if we stay here much longer. She knows that we will die if we try to take the same route back up the ridge line to the North Fork Trail. She also knows that what I am about to suggest leads to almost certain death. But she also knows something else. She knows that I am her only hope. Is that not right, Little Mother?"

"You are the only light in the darkness," Megan said, her voice a strangled whisper.

Cheobawn smiled at her reassuringly and then she turned to Tam.

"I shall not tell you what waits for us out there. You would not follow me if I did. But Megan knows. She only sees it as a shadow where I see it clearly. She will not go lightly into the jaws of the mountain. It is a terrible thing that I am asking her to do. She needs your help. I need your help. I need you to keep her calm. I need you to keep her sane. This is the game of Battle Trail, only this time, it is deadly serious."

"We need to know what is coming at us so that we can fight it," Tam said, shaking his head stubbornly.

"When and if we must fight, I will give you ample warning," Cheobawn said firmly. "If I fall, keep going west." Cheobawn's mind shied away from that possibility, refusing to curse her Luck by dwelling on the worst outcome. She had plucked the thread where she died out here on the mountain and ugly things happened to her Pack at its end. If she could get Megan closer to Home Dome, perhaps the shadows in the older girl's mind would lift and she could take control of the Pack if Cheobawn fell. Otherwise they were all going to die. "Head west until you hit a road or trail and follow it home," she repeated.

"Why can't we take the North Fork Trail?" Alain whined desperately.

Cheobawn looked at him sadly. She understood his desperation. She could feel the nut paste sitting uneasily on his stomach. She could feel his weak and watery muscles. She could feel his exhaustion bleeding out from around his internal walls. She did not have the heart to tell him about the mass of glasslizards streaming up the ridge-line in search of summer dens, their numbers their only defense against the battalions of predators, large and small, coming down the mountain to graze on their bounty, effectively cutting off the Pack's retreat.

"This is how it must be," she said, rising to her feet and slinging her pack onto her back, then sliding her stick into the loop on her belt. "I will take point. Connor will take rear guard. He is the least sick, having eaten the fewest berries. You will do everything I do, run when I run, step where I step. Hang on to your weapons, no matter what. I cannot guarantee that you will not have to fight your way clear, somewhere down this road. To tell you the truth, I cannot care. All of my mind will be focused on staying alive. If you stay at my back, perhaps you too will live. Trust in your own Luck, if you cannot trust in mine. Make no sound until we are safe inside the dome. Is that clear?"

Tam wanted to argue. He looked to Megan for support, but Megan could only look at the sky and shudder.

Cheobawn moved closer to her alpha male, touching his hand to gain his attention.

"You must trust me," she said softly, for his ears only. "But more importantly, you must trust yourself. It was you who walked into the playground this morning and chose Megan and me. Trust in that."

Tam nodded, looking sick, grim, and very frightened.

Cheobawn spun around and headed for the tunnel through the giant grass. She gave the glen one last check as she passed through it, looking for stray pieces of equipment. They would leave nothing, for they had very little and any of that might save their lives before the day was done.

Chapter Eight

The tunnel through the grass, cleared that morning, made her passage out of the grove much faster than the passage in. Cheobawn broke free of the confining stalks and splashed across the deep pool up onto dry ground. Waiting for her Pack, she paused on the bank and listened to the movement of life on the mountain. The map in Tam's pocket burned brightly in her head.

A gang of fuzzies fed upon the hapless laggards of the glass-lizard flock not far behind them. It was the way of things out in the world, that so much excess life would attract the predators. Without the intoxication of the berries, she would have remembered that.

No Pack purposefully confronted a fuzzy gang. They might be able to kill a few but the fuzzies had the advantage of numbers. How many, she could not tell. Fuzzies presented themselves upon the ambient as a single organism. Unable to count the individuals in this gang, she had to guess by the size of their psi footprint. More than twenty. Less than a hundred.

Cheobawn did not mention the fuzzies to her friends, the tiny carnivores not being the biggest threat to them at that moment. The band of tiny predators would ignore them with easier prey at hand, at least for now, but she had no wish to test that hypothesis.

Tam came out of the tunnel first, pulling Megan behind him. Alain came next, Connor close behind, watching him. Alain's feet slipped on the stones in the pool. Connor's hand was there, on his elbow, steadying him. Cheobawn flinched away from the sight, not wanting to see how desperate their plight was, right from the start.

She turned and tested the ambient, clearing her mind of all else.

The Pack could not return the way they had come so they must find a new path. She lifted her face and felt the wind on her cheek. Using that to set a heading that would leave a scent trail least likely to attract fuzzy attention, she ran.

The place of the first bright beacon in the ambient was time sensitive and time was slipping away from her. She needed to be fast but she needed to be silent and this hampered her speed. They had to be as invisible as possible. A startled flight of birds, the warning scream of a treehopper, any alarm in the forest at all would bring them to the notice of the larger predators.

The thick brush around the tubegrass grove opened up and became a longpine forest. The grassy understory was easy to navigate. All you had to do was watch for deadfalls and other random tree debris that might trip up an already wobbly child. Cheobawn planned every footfall with care, scanning the visible terrain and mapping their path. The ambient told her of hidden animals and their nests and burrows. All of this affected her route forward. Hundreds of paths, thousands of threads, all of them streaming through her mind at once. It came close to overwhelming her. She drank the energy of the mountain and used it to reinforce her link to the ambient. The world became bright and sharply focused.

Then, between one step and the next, Bear Under the Mountain took her into his great jaws and made her his own. The line that separated child from mountain disappeared.

Cheobawn had never done this before. Not on this scale. Her mind filled with confusing sensory input that she had no time to decipher. She lost track of things. She lost track of time. She lost track of the Pack behind her. Too much slipped out of her control so she fought for the one thing that mattered. She clung to the idea of the bright place in the ambient that promised survival.

Her feet danced over the ground. Was she stealing the mountain's energy or was she infusing it with her own? She could not tell. All she knew for certain was that every motion moved the world under her feet and gave her what she needed. It was a dance she was powerless to stop.

She did not want it to stop. She would let the mountain use her for its own purposes as long as it danced her all the way back to the dome

Connor chirped like a pine cricket. She ran on, having forgotten what that meant. He chirped again. Cheobawn came to a halt, her hand up, *stop* on her fingers. She let go of the ambient and turned.

Connor scowled at her, anger having replaced his fear. Alain bent over, trying desperately not to throw up. Tam had a tight grip on Megan's hand. Both of them looked ill and pale. Megan glanced quickly up at the sky and then looked away, shuddered.

Cheobawn followed the direction of her gaze. It was not the setting sun that concerned their Alpha Ear the most. Something in the sky above the rise of the mountain had become a more pressing danger.

Yes, did I not say it, Cheobawn thought to herself. *All the mountain moves against us.*

Drink. Eat. Very little, Cheobawn signed. She drank, sipping from her waterskin but she did not eat. The energy of the mountain was all her body craved.

The mountain pressed at her mind, reminding her that they had no time to wait for Alain to recover. Stowing her waterskin, Cheobawn made a sharp motion with her hand and then turned.

She ran.

The terrain sloped gradually upwards. It was not steep but it was enough of a rise to tax her leg muscles and make them burn. Cheobawn sucked down great draughts of the mountain's power to ease the ache.

Towards the top of the ridge her heart began to pound in earnest. She could not tell if it was from exertion or fear.

The things in the sky had seen them.

She put out one last bit of speed and then skidded to a halt under the twisted branches of an ancient scrub pine that grew on the edge of a ravine. The hand signal she flashed at the Pack coming up behind her was half warning and half a command for absolute stillness.

Cheobawn lifted her face to the sky and listened with all her senses.

Sound became brittle and unnaturally loud. She could hear the shift of every needle as the light breeze caught at the boughs of the tree above her head. One of her Pack coughed softly behind her. The sound berated her and her ruthless heart. It hurt them to run, that sound said. Cheobawn pushed that thought from her mind.

Somewhere high overhead, a pair of sky hunters circled lazily, waiting for prey to do something fatally stupid. Cheobawn thought she could hear the sound of the wind and feel the wind as it flowed across the vast spread of their leathery wings. She shook her head, half expecting to hear the long spines along their chins clack together as if they were her own but surely that was her imagination. One called to the other, telling him of the children hiding under the pine tree. For a moment, Cheobawn could not breathe.

Megan moaned in fear. Cheobawn looked back, not at her friend but at Tam, reminding him of his one job. Tam scowled at Cheobawn as he took the older girl's hand and tried to redirect her attention, whispering something in her ear. After a moment, Megan calmed.

Cheobawn knew better than anyone what that must have cost in effort. Megan's psi skills were highly honed. She surely must have sensed the forces that moved against them, exposed as they were, here on this rocky ridge.

Steeling her heart against her friend's pain, Cheobawn glanced to the west. The sun was settling inexorably towards the horizon. She wanted to keep moving. Time was slipping away from her.

Wait, whispered Bear Under the Mountain.

Cheobawn tried to stay calm but the sky hunters knew they were here. She could feel the weight of their attention. This scrub pine would not keep the Pack safe if the sky hunters decided to take them.

Wanting to be ready, she turned to studying the way in front of them. The slope was steep and treacherous. Low growing brush covered what scree and rock outcroppings did not. When it came time to move, they would have to take it at high speed.

It was going to take the agility of a bennelk. Pulling her hook from her belt, she grasped it just below the blade before turning to look back at Tam. All three boys had their eyes riveted to her. She pointed down the slope then signed her instructions.

Use your sticks for balance. I will take this fast. Follow. Copy me. Do not slow down or you will die, she said. The boys pulled their bladed sticks off their backs. Even Megan complied. Cheobawn looked from one worried face to the next. Her Pack did not protest. Cheobawn nodded in satisfaction and turned, stepping to the edge.

Taking the slope was suicide with the sky hunters watching but worse things waited for them down in that valley. Cheobawn drank deep from the mountain until everything took on the bright, hard-edge glow and then waited for their fortunes to change.

The monster moving down the valley met a herd of grunters. Squealing in terror, they scattered. The sky hunters spotted a small calf. Chittering in anticipation, they flattened their wings against their sides and dove.

Cheobawn was already leaping off the valley rim onto the first rock outcropping. She did not pause, leaping again almost instantly to clear the stone for those coming behind her. One stone to the next. She hit a scree patch half way down. The loose stones slipped under her feet. She rode them, dancing from one to the next, down to the bottom before leaping clear to land on a downed tree trunk. She did not turn around to check on her Pack. The sound of shifting stone reassured her. The tree trunk acted as a bridge that took her over the impassable wall of dense brush that marked the edge of a cedar grove.

At the fractured base of the tree, she leaped clear, landing on the soft duff under an ancient giant. She allowed herself the luxury of one quick glance over her shoulder. Megan ran down the trunk, Tam following close, then came Alain and Connor.

Satisfied, Cheobawn turned and sprinted through the massive trees. The dark thing was so close she could almost smell it. But surely this too was her imagination.

In the heart of the grove a giant cedar, old and rotted at its core had fallen recently. It had not gone down easily. The tree had torn a great hole in the earth and half the stones it had counted on as anchors for its immense weight still remained lodged in its roots.

The minute she saw it, Cheobawn knew why she was here and what she had to do. She skidded in the duff at the top of the pit and let her momentum carry her over the lip and down into its depths. At the bottom she tumbled towards the dark cave formed by the overhanging rootball. Scrambling on hands and knees for the last few feet, she turned and pressed her back against the wall of the hole, her hook clutched in both hands.

Tam made it to the bottom of the pit in three great leaps before he turned and caught Megan as she ran down the slope in a barely controlled fall. Tam pushed her behind him and caught Alain, whose fall from the top threatened broken bones. Connor danced down the slope behind him, his descent almost delicate in comparison.

Her Pack crawled into the cave and mimicked her stance, crouched, backs against the damp earth, blades at the ready.

Do not breathe, she signed, with a snap of her fingers. Tam glared at her. Cheobawn had no room in her mind to care.

Something was coming. Cheobawn watched the small bit of forest outside their cave and tried to prepare herself. The ambient filled with images of teeth, claws, and insatiable hunger. *Run before my awful power,* it declared into the forest gloom, as if it owned all the world. Perhaps it did. The mountain's ambient colluded with the monster's psi and lied to her senses. Every particle of her body wanted to run away. The need was irrational.

Irrational. She realized suddenly that she knew of this thing. Bhotta. She tried to recite the bhotta lesson to herself but terror scrambled her mind, a terror she could not shake. The lessons said that most of this terror was the construct of a psi predator at the apex of the food chain but no lesson could prepare you for the way the tendrils of its manufactured terror seeped into the mind and made the heart race.

Cheobawn felt something else bleeding into the ambient. Unguarded emotions. Bhottas received as well as they sent. The Pack was betraying their own hiding place. Cheobawn snapped her head around to glare at her friends.

Quiet! Do not think! she signed furiously. She looked at Megan. The older girl had her hands over her ears, her eyes squeezed shut. Cheobawn glared at Tam.

Quiet her, she signed forcefully.

Tam hissed, his fury at her lack of mercy apparent but he obeyed, reaching out to pull Megan close. He curled his hands around her neck, burying his fingertips in her hair as he pressed his cheek against hers, whispering a mantra in her ear, though the sound came to Cheobawn's ears as nothing more than the hiss of the wind in the treetops.

Cheobawn's eyes widened in surprise. Tam's thumbs hovered over the arteries in Megan's neck. The hold, while disturbingly intimate, was logical and well considered. If Megan did not quiet, Tam could press his thumbs into her neck, cutting off the flow of blood into her brain, inducing unconsciousness with little effort. Surely this was not intuition on Tam's part. Someone had taught him that hold. In a remote corner of Cheobawn's mind, she wondered if the Fathers kept secrets that even the Mothers had not discovered.

Cheobawn tore her gaze away, returning her attention to the dark monster that was busy turning their minds into nightmare. The lessons said this was how a bhotta hunted but classroom lessons had not prepared her for the power of the psi wave that preceded it. It was a ploy meant to flush the lesser creatures from their dens and into its jaws. She closed her eyes but that only made the urge to run worse. She opened her eyes and stared at the ground beneath her feet, shuddering under the strain of trying to keep the bhotta out of her skull.

Suddenly, the ambient went numb. Cheobawn's head snapped up, her eyes wide. This could mean only one thing. The bhotta was close. Too close. Surely it must smell them. The void in the ambient was its trap, the lie to entice the unwary to leap in the wrong direction, into the massive jaws full of deadly teeth. The prey, fleeing the terror in the ambient, ran towards the dark promise and died.

Cheobawn brought her hook up and waited for the lizard to find them. She could feel Megan shielding her mind with every ounce of her ability and was thankful for that but doubtful that it would save them. The emptiness pressed in on them, crushing the will to live. Cheobawn felt her heart flutter, as the bhotta's psi field caught at her mind.

Unaccountably, she felt rage ignite inside her. She had followed this thread, this version of one of their futures, because it had promised survival. Was it a lie, that bright spot in the ambient? Had she misunderstood its message? What was the point of coming here, if they were to die as a bhotta's supper? What was she missing? This was stupid and unfair. She grit her teeth, angry with the bhotta, with Bear Under the Mountain, with herself.

No, she thought furiously at the ambient, no, I will not go quietly into your jaws. The rage bloomed, leaping up to burn away the bhotta's version of reality and replace it with her own. Cheobawn lifted her face to the unseen sky and snarled silently.

Two could play this game. She set her mental fingers into the fabric of the world and radiated nothingness with all her might. She lied to the ambient. She told it that the cave was full of darkness and nothing else and at its core lay something so powerful it could eat the world. She built the illusion in her mind until even she believed it.

Something massive moved through the underbrush almost directly over their heads. She heard it with only a corner of her mind. The rest of her was locked in the illusion of being something terrible hidden under all that Nothing.

It took forever for the sound of its long body to slither past them. Huge. This explained the excitement of the sky hunters far overhead. A bhotta this big was sure to flush out more than it could catch. The sky hunters merely had to wait and pick the animals off as they fled in panic. *Not today,* she thought at them fiercely. *You will not feast on my bones this day.*

The sky hunters ignored her, moving down the mountain in the bhotta's wake.

Chapter Nine

They did not die. This surprised her. She waited, listening, her fist held up to hold her Pack in place. The bhotta moved slowly downhill. Eventually, the sky hunters moved out of range. When it seemed that the time was again right, she signaled to her Pack to follow and clambered out of the hole. The stink of bhotta hung heavy on the air. She pressed her hand to her nose to keep from sneezing and ran on, the Pack on her heels.

The warm valley air flowed up the mountain, taking their scent away from the bhotta's nose. She counted on that flow. It was one of the key pieces in her strategic game of hunter and hunted but she knew that the wind would begin to shift, on towards dusk and betray them. Time was her enemy.

Wait, whispered Bear.

Cheobawn skidded to a halt, confused. The overwhelming need to race towards home was an excruciatingly painful feeling. Once again the next bright place lay just beyond her reach, dark.

She stamped her foot in frustration. Wait? Wait for what?

One of the children clicked a query behind her. She held up her hand, wishing them silent as she put all her energy into listening for the moment that would tell her it was safe to move.

A bull fenelk bugle somewhere south of their position. Cheobawn found it in the ambient and tasted its mood. Nervous that the sky hunters circled high overhead, it headed downhill towards the southern forests where it would spend the night. She followed it in her mind as it strode beneath an ancient blackoak, its horns laid flat along its back, its tusks up and ready for anything that would be so foolish as to attack it.

A dubeh leopard lifted its head from where it rested on a blackoak branch, watching the elk. The giant cat was on its way up to the needletree forest where the grunters grazed in the evenings. Cheobawn's heart twisted painfully in her chest. She and her demi-Pack stood in its path.

The leopard was in no hurry. It rose to its feet and stalked the fenelk along the high branches. If they hurried, they would avoid the leopard. She turned towards home but the bright spot in the ambient was not in front of her. It was somewhere uphill. Cheobawn peered up the slope but saw nothing, felt nothing. She did not understand the need for the detour.

Tam clicked another query.

Cheobawn looked back at him. *Dubeh leopard,* she signed. *Wait.*

Tam's eyes widened.

She checked the dubeh once more. It had grown bored with its game and now paced the trees in their direction.

She looked towards home again and took a step in that direction. All the threads in her mind died and turned dark.

Fine.

Cheobawn flashed Tam a grim look and turned to face up the slope. Her first step told her she was going in the right direction. She began to run in earnest. Alain groaned behind her. She did not pause or slow her speed. A dubeh was not something any of them could face.

The tracks of many grunters crossed the slope just below a vast expanse of scree. She stopped and turned. Her friends staggered to a stop. Pointing towards the deep hoof prints, she signed. *Do what I do.*

Then she ran alongside the hoof prints for a hundred paces before leaping away downhill. Tam danced over the grunter trail, following her lead.

When the dubeh turned to go hunting in earnest, it would find their scent trail and follow it. The grunter spoor would remind it that it was hungry and that humans were a poor meal, by comparison.

The next bright place in the ambient pulled her onward. Cheobawn did not slow her pace. She gradually worked her way down the hill, mindful of her exhausted companions.

The roosting tree of a flock of carrion lizards blocked their way south. She turned west and ran on.

The black water bogs lay in that direction. She did not want to cross the bogs. She tried to veer north and west, hoping to take a path between the cliffs and the vast pools of stinking black water but the threads of their future died inside her mind. Cheobawn tried to sense what blocked the way. A hive of stinging nasties infested the rocks there and a fenelk mother and her small calf stood dozing just beyond that. She backtracked and found another way around the pool, picking her footing on ground that oozed black mud if you stood too long in any one spot. They were now in the heart of the bogs, a place not even the most experienced trackers ever went.

Bear Under the Mountain danced around her, enticing her on. She snarled at him, tired of his games. She did not want to be here. She wanted to veer north, away from the sucking mud and the clouds of tiny biting flies, but rock slides blocked that retreat. She thought about heading south and west towards the well traveled South Road where they would have been unhindered by rough terrain and thick vegetation but black water blocked every turn.

Life on the mountain was in motion, pressing at her psi sense. She pressed back, pushing with all her might at things that threatened to cross in front of them and cut off their only route, wishing them to pause, as the dubeh had done, to stay, to turn and find another direction.

Sight and psi sense began to blur dangerously. Reality twisted inside her head. She moved the world by running. Running was all she could do.

Cheobawn tried to stay focused by making it into a game. Pluck the threads of their future, pick the strongest, and follow it until it ran out. Choose another. She would adjust direction, run for a while until the thread ran out in her mind, then she would change directions to follow the next. It was like navigating in a pitch black room. She knew this game. The Mothers played it with their daughters as soon as they could walk. Find the dolly. No coming out until you found dolly. Cheobawn really hated dollies.

Another bright spot in the ambient approached. At just the right moment, she pivoted and raced straight up the slope towards a point where the ridge jutted out into the valley. Here the rock had collapsed under its own weight, leaving a lone stone spire standing sentinel over an expanse of rock slides dotted with patches of vegetation trying to find a foothold in the unstable ground.

The sound of snuffling and the click of claws on the loose

rock above them greeted her ears as she clambered up to the base of the spire. The sound was faint and she heard it only because she was expecting it. They were nearly out of time, once again.

Climb, she signed frantically. She did not wait to see that they obeyed. She jammed her hooked stick into the loops on her belt to free both hands. Jumping up as high as she could reach, her fingertips caught a knob of rock as a handhold. Using her momentum, she swung her knee up to wedge the toe of her boot into a crack. From this precarious perch, she pulled herself up to reach for the next irregularity in the face of the rock.

Taking the holds dangerously fast, the climb took less than a minute but it felt like forever. A large flat stone crowned the pinnacle. She threw her arm over the lip and clawed at the rough stone as she inched over the rim on her belly. Safe at last, she collapsed and tried to get her breath back.

Was it fear or fatigue that turned her muscles to jelly? It was hard to tell. She had not taken a drink since well before the bhotta and the last food she had eaten had long since disappeared, making her belly feel hollow. Cheobawn pulled all the power she could handle out of the mountain's reserve, postponing the needs of her body for some future time.

When she thought she could handle it, she crawled to the edge to help the next person up. Megan was almost to the rim. Cheobawn spread herself flat and pulled the older girl up the last few feet by her belt. Alain was next, with Tam climbing by his side, though there was little Tam could do if Alain lost a hold point and fell.

She risked a glance up the slope but dense brush blocked her view. Whatever it was, it had caught their scent. A deep, excited moan came from just beyond a thicket of thornberries.

The hairs on the back of her neck stood on end.

She grabbed Alain's hand, Megan grabbed the other and between the two of them, they hauled him over the rim. He collapsed face down on the tiny plateau nearly sobbing with exhaustion as Tam pulled himself up and whirled around to reach down towards Connor.

The youngest boy was still too far down. He was having a hard time of it for some reason. Every gain up the rock face twisted his face in agony. Cheobawn measured the distance between him and the ground and then checked up-slope. They were out of time. A large prehensile nose pushed its way clear of the greenery and sniffed deeply. Massive shoulders parted the stalks as the rest of the animal followed its nose towards the desperate Pack.

A treebear. The thing was as tall as a grown man at the shoulder and standing on its hind feet it surely would be taller than three grown men. They were good climbers, these animals, if their claws could find a purchase.

Cheobawn felt sick. She may have doomed them, bringing them up here with nowhere to retreat.

The treebear rose on its hind legs and lifted its nose high in the air. It had not spotted them yet but surely it would soon. What it lacked in vision and psi abilities it more than made up for with its nose.

Megan pushed Cheobawn out of the way and lay down on her belly, inching forward as far as she could. Alarmed, Cheobawn grabbed the older girl's ankles and braced her heels against the rock, holding on as tight as she could. Alain did the same for Tam as Tam leaned out over the edge, though Alain looked as weak as a baby and probably could not hold on for long if Tam started to fall.

Connor came up at last, clawing his way over the bodies of

his friends. Cheobawn grabbed them all, pulled them away from the edges, and pressed them down into the stone. Alain shuddered, trying to smother a cough with his fist, his exhausted lungs betraying him. There was so little room in the center of the cap stone they were forced to overlap arms and legs, forming a solid ball of child flesh. Cheobawn spread herself thin around the edge of the ball, hugging Megan with her legs and Connor with her arms. Every moment or so, she lifted her head just enough to keep track of the bear.

The treebear whuffed deeply and dropped back down on all four feet. Rocks shifted and skittered under its weight. Its claws, large enough to rip open dead trees in search of honeybuzzer nests and treehopper dens, gave it an odd, toed-in gait as it clambered down the loose stones, swinging its head from side to side to catch their scent. Cheobawn watched as it approached the base of their roost and then disappeared below them.

Now was when she would find out how good their Luck was. She buried her nose in the small of Connor's back, held her breath, and waited.

All sound of movement stopped right below them. The snuffing intensified. That could mean only one thing. It knew they were up here. Cheobawn cursed their rotten Luck and tried to figure out where she had gone wrong. On the surface, walking right up under the nose of a treebear with the breeze at their backs seemed suicidal. But getting above its nose should have confused it. If they had truly been blessed, the bear should have followed their backtrail down the slope.

Claws scraped against the rock face and the stone under them quaked slightly. The bear had not been fooled. It was trying to climb. It paced the base of the spire, trying every crack and crevice with a tenacious thoroughness, circling once, twice, and then again a third time, the sound of its excited whuffing marking its progress. Occasionally it would find a purchase for its claws but the stone was too brittle. They listened to the tiny pops as the rock fractured under the bear's weight, the surface of the spire shedding flakes of itself, the chips clattering down the steep incline to add themselves to the already unstable scree.

The treebear's frustrated moan gave her hope. What had afforded small children a toe hold was not enough for something as massive as a treebear. Perhaps Luck was still on their side. Cheobawn lifted her head and then clutched frantically at anything within reach as the stone shuddered, then shuddered again.

For a moment she thought it was an earthquake. Then it hit her. The treebear was trying to knock the stone spire over using its massive strength.

The stones shuddered once more.

She had not thought she could be more afraid than she already was but true terror exploded in her mind like fire, stripping away any illusion of control she might have thought she had over what lay in her core. Adrenaline fueled a firestorm of psi that caught her up in its pressure wave and blew her out into the world.

For a moment, the world became nothing but light and sound and she was the formless thing unraveling at its core. She clutched at the fabric of reality, trying to find an anchor point.

Cheobawn became a frightened ball of children, but she could not hang onto that thought, the winds of her fear too strong. In succession, she became a stone spire, then a treebear intent on toppling this great stone tree.

Cheobawn could not stop the storm that was blowing her away from herself. She became the stones and bones of a ridge line that held back the weight of half a mountain. She became the mountain, perpetual snowfields on her crown, the forest living flesh upon her flanks, the bones of her roots sunk into a hot mass of the plastic rock that seethed restlessly under the weight of its rigid shell.

Not even a planet could contain her. She was preparing to leap off into the vacuum of space after becoming the ball of living rock caught up in the tyranny of a star's orbit when sanity returned. Little girls did not belong in the darkness between stars. Little girls belonged in little bodies. She released her hold on the expanding bubble of psi energy and sank back towards the fragile vessel meant to contain her life spark.

Cheobawn remembered, as she let go of the place where she existed as a mountain, that she was still in mortal danger. As she contracted down to tree size, she found the treebear, standing on its hind legs, front paws planted against a puny mound of rock. She settled into it, pulling its life close around her like a warm blanket on a cold morning.

Cheobawn found herself staring at her paws, confused. Why was she trying to tip this stone? Then the faintest smell of blood reminded her. She had treed a thing without a name and it was wounded. The promise of an easy dinner was hard to ignore. She reared back and hit the spire one more time, putting the weight of her massive shoulders behind that blow. Though stone ground against stone, nothing big seemed to be shaking loose. It was very frustrating. She lifted her nose high and tasted the air, her mouth watering, imagining warm furry bodies struggling in her jaws, the blood flowing hot, bones cracking.

No!

Revulsion flooded her mind. Cheobawn shied away, landing on all fours. She shook her head to clear it of the thoughts that buzzed around inside her like a swarm of flying nasties. She did not want to eat the nameless ones. She loved them. Didn't she? She moaned, rocking from paw to paw, love and hunger mixed up in her mind.

A fernhen clucked somewhere downhill, a welcome distraction, and Cheobawn lifted her nose to catch its scent. Hens meant eggs. She loved eggs. She turned and scrambled down the scree, putting distance between herself and the unease that clung to the tall spire.

Someone was shaking her arm. She opened her eyes. Tam was crouched over her.

Sleeping? Really! he signed, a look of astonished disbelief on his face. *This is not a stroll through the garden. We can relax later,* his fingers scolded.

Cheobawn sat up and scrubbed her hands roughly over her face. Had she fainted? Had it been a dream?

Where is the treebear? she queried with the flick of a finger. Tam looked over his shoulder and clicked softly. Alain was flat on his belly peering over the edge. He looked up at the sound. Tam repeated her question.

Gone down into the trees, headed into the swamp, Alain signed. Cheobawn rose to her knees and looked over the side. It was truly gone. Once again, Luck had smiled upon them.

She turned and considered each member of her pack, biting her lip. Whether a dream or a prescient vision, her foray out to the edge of the world had told her one thing. She signed at Tam and Megan to watch the sky. She touched their bladed sticks and pointed up to reinforce that idea. Then she turned to Connor.

Are you hurt? she signed.

It is nothing, he signed back. She did not believe him, but she also did not believe he was trying to be stoic. He was angry with her.

Liar, she signed. *Show me.*

Connor scowled at her and then reluctantly answered.

Wet boots, he signed with a grimace.

Explain, she signed, puzzled. They all had wet boots. The liners were designed to compensate for that.

Sore foot, he signed with a shrug. She frowned at him. It was surely more than just being footsore. She calculated the distance left to go, calling up Tam's map to compare it with her own internal map. It was still far. Too far. Doubly far if one of them was lame.

Show me, she insisted.

No. I will be alright, he signed with an angry flick of his fingers.

She reached for his boot. Connor tried to bat her hands away but Tam reached out and caught hold of his wrist.

Follow orders, the older boy signed. Connor pressed his lips together to contain his anger and then unlaced one of his boots. Cheobawn helped him pull it off. What she saw gave her pause.

Where is your liner? she signed with a sinking feeling.

Lost. At the pool, he signed.

The boots were cut big to accommodate the thickness of the liner. Without it, the foot had a tendency to slip around a lot inside the boot, causing abrasions and blisters. Soaking the foot and the leather in water exacerbated the problem a thousand fold. The sole of his foot, the back of his heel and the bottom of every toe were solid blisters. Most of them had burst and now oozed pink fluid. It was like looking at raw meat.

It had not been a dream.

Why didn't you say something? she asked, letting her frustration show on her face.

You did not wait, Connor signed, a look of angry accusation on his face. *You left me. Without looking behind. What was I supposed to do?* Connor's body shook with his outrage.

Tam touched Connor's shoulder but the smaller boy shook his hand off, his eyes locked with hers.

She could not deny it. Connor knew even if Tam did not. She bit her lip against the words that wanted to spill out of her heart. She had forgotten him. At the pool. In the tubegrass grove. She had nearly left without him.

I was scared. It will not happen again. Promise, she signed. Connor glared at her, unmollified. His anger was justifiable. She did not tell him she might have to break that promise again soon.

What can we do? signed Megan

I can make it, Connor signed, grabbing his boot. *Keep going.*

No, Cheobawn said. His foot would be a bleeding wound in another click. The smell of blood would have every predator on the mountain on their trail. She considered leaving him here and coming back for him but she knew he would not live to see the morning. There were sky hunters large enough to pluck grown treehoppers from the top of the forest canopy. What chance did a small boy have? They could stick together, try to hold the rock spire all night and hike out in the morning but the thought of that made her insides turn to water. More people than just this Pack would be dead when morning came. They needed to get back before the Fathers sent out search parties. The Fathers would not risk their lives for four foolish children, but they might be induced to come after her, Mora's truedaughter.

Cheobawn looked around at the faces of her friends. Alain was in trouble, lips pale and eyes deeply shadowed. Tam, though not as bad, still looked a little green. Megan was the least impacted, physically, but her mental state kept her close to the edge of control. Cheobawn rubbed her forehead, trying to push back the ambient of the mountain that threatened to crush her.

Things were going wrong. The Luck was shifting. She had walked the world in treebear's body. That blackout did not speak well of her own mental state. It had been so easy, leaping out her body, becoming that which could not be dominated. Dead easy. What if she left and never came back? Would they let the mountain take her body, thinking her dead? Her mind shied away from that unspeakable thought.

They had to get off this rock and keep going. She looked around. Surely there must be something around them that they could use to bandage his foot. Next time, she thought, we will bring extra liners and a medkit and trail rations that could be eaten on the go and day packs instead of gleaner baskets, even though the gleaner baskets could hold fragile things without crushing them. Fragile things like eggs.

Cheobawn looked up, grinning.

I am an idiot, she said pulling off her pack. She pulled a handful of damp moss out of its depths and began arranging it into a foot shaped pad. She kept adding more and more moss until the thickness seemed right. Tam, understanding the point of her crafting, handed her Connor's boot. She slid the pad in and then added a little more around the edges, taking care to pad the toes. When it seemed right, she handed the boot back to Connor.

Connor tried to put it on. The pain made him moan. Resting had not helped his foot. It was starting to swell.

Cheobawn lifted her head to taste the ambient. Time was sliding away. She moved to take the boot but Tam grabbed it first. He shoved Connor onto his back and grabbed his ankle.

Hold him down, Tam signed at Megan.

Megan moved to kneel over Connor's head, pressing his shoulders down onto the rock with all her weight.

Hold his knee, Tam told Cheobawn. Cheobawn sat down and pulled Connor's leg into her lap, his other knee pressed against her back.

Tam looked into Connor's eyes and made sure he could see his fingers when he signed.

This will hurt. A lot.

Connor nodded.

The next two minutes were the worst of Cheobawn's short life. Connor did not make a sound as Tam forced his foot back into the boot but Cheobawn could feel him stiffen and jerk with the pain. Cheobawn was crying when it was done, her tears matching those that streamed down Connor's cheeks. The small boy lay, pale and trembling as Tam scooped the rest of the moss out of her pack and stuffed it tightly around Connor's ankle. When he was satisfied, he tightened the laces, securing them again in the top of the boot.

Tight? Tam's fingers asked, his fingers catching at Connor's attention. Connor sat up and rubbed the sweat out of his eyes and flicked a finger. Tam repeated his question.

Too tight, Connor signed with a grimace.

Good, Tam nodded, *No movement. No blood on the ground.* He used the hunter's sign for an animal bleeding out, perhaps as a warning to Connor to remind him of his danger.

The others looked grim at that reminder. Good, Cheobawn thought, good to think such things when you are running for your life. She slipped her pack back on while she tested the threads of their future in her mind. One of the threads seemed promising. She slid over the edge and began the climb down.

Tam came next, leading Connor down as he tested the limits

of his padded foot. He seemed to be more steady, the moss padding easing the pain a bit.

Alain came next. He lost a toe hold not far from the bottom and dropped the last two meters with Tam breaking his fall. Megan jumped down last. Cheobawn waited for them to sort themselves out. When she had their attention, she lifted her fingers.

Not far. Around two clicks, she guessed.

None of them looked happy at the news. Two clicks might as well have been twenty. The rest on the spire had not helped them.

Cheobawn shook her head, looking away. There was nothing more she could do for them. The mountain wanted her attention.

She turned and ran.

Chapter Ten

The weight of their exhaustion beat at Cheobawn from behind. It began to influence her decisions. She closed her eyes and tried to find a path that would spare Alain and Connor anymore pain.

Following a thread that wound its way around the northern edge of a marshy bog, careful to keep them out of the sucking mud traps that lay under the pools of still water, she stepped one step too far down a thread that suddenly had no future. Cheobawn stopped and tried to find a place to go but all the threads of all their futures faded and died in her mind.

The world had turned into chaos.

She stood, swaying in the ambient winds, afraid to move. Her Pack stopped where they stood, grateful for the rest, their distress hanging in the air, pressing at her mind. She tried to block them out and clear her mind but her own exhaustion sucked at her will and clouded her mind.

She did not look around. *This is where pity gets you,* she thought. Trying to spare them, she had led them into a dead end.

Cheobawn lifted her face towards the fading light, sank deeper into the flesh of the mountain, and listened.

Death stalks you, the great mountain bear whispered. Her mind shied away from that, her heart fluttering in panic. They had stayed too long on the top of the stone spire. Now something bad had caught up with them.

Home Dome she imagined with all her might into Bear's chaos. But chaos had closed that door. Home Dome was unattainable. *No, no,* she thought, *we are so close. It cannot be far.*

Two clicks, if that. Rested and healthy, they could be home in their beds by dark. But they were anything but rested.

Cheobawn turned to look at her friends. They looked haggard. She was surprised that Alain and Connor were still standing. Tam was helping Alain with his waterskin, insisting the boy drink. Connor swayed where he stood. He probably would have fallen but Megan had her arm around his waist, offering a steadying hand.

Drink, eat little, Tam's fingers flashed the order to everyone. Connor's fingers fumbled clumsily as he reached for his water skin.

Cheobawn realized then that while she had been racing them across the mountain, Tam had been using every trick he knew to keep the Pack on their feet and on her tail. Had she trusted implicitly that he would figure out a way to keep his Pack alive?

She had assumed so much, a fools mistake, that. They should not have lived so long yet here they were. But to what purpose? They were about to die. Was it cowardice or arrogance that made her think she could defy the will of the Goddess, running them to the ends of their strength, having only postponed the inevitable? She wanted to cry.

Tam felt her eyes on him and looked up. He saw something in her face

What is wrong? he asked.

Cheobawn bit her lip. Would it be kinder to let death sneak up on them or tell them now so that they might prepare? Her eyes sought Megan's. The older girl was looking at her, an odd stillness on her young face.

What do you see? signed Megan, though Cheobawn was certain she already knew the answer.

I am blind. The way forward is gone, Cheobawn signed.

Clarify, snapped Tam's fingers.

We move, we die. We stay here, we die. Something is wrong, Cheobawn signed.

Tam shook his head, refusing to accept that as an answer. Cheobawn looked at him helplessly.

Listen, Megan signed, catching their attention. *Something comes at us from behind.*

Why didn't you say so before? Tam's fingers asked.

The way forward was always more deadly. Sorry, Megan grimaced. *We were outrunning it until now.* They both turned an inquiring looked at Cheobawn.

Cheobawn cast her attention down their back trail. She flinched, feeling sick. The fuzzies from the grove had grown tired of glasslizards. Picking up the scent of humans at the grove, they had followed. All the obstacles that slowed the children to a snails pace, forcing them into great curving detours, these things meant nothing to the small, light-bodied predators. They were coming, straight and true and they were coming fast.

Cheobawn suppressed her panic and tried to sense the mood of the gang and then wished she hadn't. The stink of human made their mouths water and their little hearts beat with excitement. They remembered human flesh. Cheobawn choked, appalled at this memory. She tried to lie to their ambient, insisting the trail was old, their quarries long gone, but they would have none of it. The scent trail was everything to the little beasts, filling their minds to the exclusion of all else. This was their nature. The gang would not stop until they had run the trail to its end. She remembered suddenly that she knew this fact. She had learned it in another lifetime, when facts were just things to memorize in the safety of a classroom. It was from her old life, before she had come outside and found that facts had teeth and claws and could eat you if you were unwise.

They were in serious trouble. A grown man could outrun them but five foot-sore kids could not. It would be a terrible death. A bhotta or a treebear or a dubeh would kill you quick. A fuzzy gang would eat you slow, one little mouthful at a time. Was it a part of her cruel Bad Luck, that she had saved them from one death only to deliver them into one more horrifying? Tam and Megan saw the despair on her face.

What? signed Tam.

Cheobawn was out of ideas. They needed to know.

Fuzzy gang. Less than a click. On our trail, Cheobawn signed.

Alain had not seen the fingersign, his eyes closed in misery. Connor's hiss of fear caught at his attention. He lifted his head to look desperately around. Signing a query, Connor answered. Cheobawn looked away from the panic that flashed in his eyes. Her own eyes found Megan's.

Megan shuddered at the news but managed to keep whatever she was feeling out of the ambient. Cheobawn smiled at her best friend, heartened that the older girl seemed to be controlling the stress of being under the threat of immanent death a little better. Somehow it made Cheobawn feel better; less alone, perhaps.

Tam's click caught at her attention. He pulled a piece of paper out of the thigh pocket of his shorts, an excited look on his face. Squinting down at it, he studied what lay there. Cheobawn moved to his side to look. It was their foray form. Tam handed it to her.

Where are we? he signed.

Cheobawn took the map and held it close to her eyes so that the lines filled her vision. She listened to the planet as it rolled through space and then rotated the map so that north pointed north. It took her a moment to sort out the lay of the land and match it to the map. Finally she had it. By the Goddess, she thought sadly, looking at the symbol for Home Dome, we were so close. She handed the map back and put her finger on the spot where they stood. Tam studied the map for a moment and then stabbed his finger on a red numbered box.

Take us there, he signed.

She scowled at the red square. This would not get them any closer to home. In fact, the detour led them uphill and away from the dome, a terrible thing to ask of the exhausted Pack.

Why? she asked.

Trust me, Tam signed. Cheobawn studied his face. This was not a plea from a desperate boy. This was Tam, invoking his authority as Alpha. Trust. Why not? They had nothing more to lose.

She smiled. The burden of getting them all home safe seemed to lift a bit.

Chapter Eleven

Cheobawn sniffed the ambient behind them. The fuzzy gang flowed across the earth like water tumbling down the mountain, surmounting each obstacle it encountered in waves of furry flesh. The Pack had no time to waste. She turned and began to run in earnest, not caring how much noise they made this time. The need for speed outweighed the need for silence.

She probed the ambient in front of them while she ran, looking for what lay under that red square on the map, to make sure she had them going in the right direction. Horror shivered up her spine, making her stumble. She twisted, barely saving herself from a tumble and felt something give in her right knee. She refused to allow it to stop her. Instead, she lied to her body, making it believe it was the mountain bear; telling her bones to be stone; telling her legs to be trees; telling her muscles that they were as powerful as the hot plastic rock in the heart of the mountain. That seemed to work, though she was careful of how she stepped afterward, fearing to test the limits of this magic.

Running up hill took everything she had inside her and all she could steal from the flesh of the mountain but it was much worse for the Pack. The ambient behind her washed red with their agony. The children crested the ridge together, staggering as the ground flattened unexpectedly beneath their feet. Cheobawn did not pause. They ran on.

She very nearly did not see the warning sign in the failing light. One last ray of sunlight broke through the trunks of the giant cedars and glinted off a thin strand suspended between a gap in the trees. She skidded to a halt, holding up her hand, and stood trembling. It was almost painful being this close to the things that lay hidden under the ferns just beyond the web.

Stinging Spider webs, she signed over her shoulder.

Tam came up the column of children to stand beside her. She pointed at the strand. He nodded.

Step exactly where I step, he signed.

Now that she knew what to look for, the webs were easier to see. She followed Tam as he sidled close to the nearest strand where it stretched between two tree trunks. She tried to remember what she knew of stinging spiders. The webs, though large, stretching from the ground to well above her head and encompassing the trunks of nearly a dozen trees, were not in and of themselves dangerous. A child could easily break through the silk. It was the things waiting in the web's heart that needed to be respected.

Tam stopped and picked up a small branch. Turning, he pointed at her hand. Cheobawn held out her right arm, puzzled. He untied the laces of her makeshift gaiter and tucked the leather lace into a pocket. Wrapping the woolsey scarf loosely around the twig, he drew back his arm and tossed it gently up and over the top of the closest web. The scarf unfurled in midair and drifted down to settle lightly on the top of the ferns ten paces beyond while the stick landed further in towards the center. A few fern fronds shuddered slightly around the stick. Cheobawn held her breath but nothing else untoward happened. Trees shed deadwood all the time, she reassured herself, a thing the spiders surely must have learned to ignore.

Tam caught her attention with a soft chirrup. Turning, he picked his way carefully around the tangled webs. Cheobawn followed, the Pack close on her heels. Tam walked the perimeter of the nest, circling around it until their back trail lay directly across from them. Cheobawn could just make out the pale spot of her woolsey scarf where it lay lightly across the tops of the ferns. She nearly laughed out loud at Tam's cleverness. He was creating a scent line through the heart of the web array. She held out her left arm, offering him her other gaiter. Tam shook his head and turned. He ran fifty paces into the forest, away from the nest and the oncoming fuzzies.

Stopping, he turned and grabbed her left arm, undoing her other gaiter.

How close? How long? he asked with the fingers of one hand as he loosened the lace with the other. Cheobawn lifter her head and listened.

Too close. Let's go, she said, trying to tug her arm free.

Stay, he signed, pulling the scarf from her arm. *Count to fifty. Then run home. No matter what happens,* he signed, reinforcing his command with a stern stare.

Cheobawn stared at him, her heart twisting in her chest. He was going to get himself killed. To save them.

Cheobawn refused to let that happen. She nodded, not so much to tell him that she agreed but to let him know she understood. She turned, touched Megan's arm and pointed her in the direction of home, trusting that the older girl's psi would kick in once clear of the threat of the spiders and lead her to safety. Megan nodded. From the look on Megan's face, Cheobawn knew the older girl was gathering up the threads of her Luck once more. Cheobawn smiled encouragingly.

Tam signed something she did not catch and then turning, ran back the way they had come.

Fifty count, Cheobawn signed insistently at Connor, *then run.* Turning, she ran after Tam.

The light was failing them. She caught up with him, stopping him with a hand on his arm. Her fingers dug deep into his flesh as the ambient whispered terrible things to her. Panic was making her heart pound in her chest and her head ache with the flush of adrenaline.

Tam turned on her, a snarl on his face. *I said stay. Get back.*

Cheobawn clung to his arm, undaunted by his rage. Out of the corner of her eye she caught the glint of something down low in the ferns near his feet. The now familiar feeling of too much power flowing through the ambient took her and held her. The world became etched in hard-edged light.

She tugged him aside instinctively, without knowing why. Her boot caught at something in the undergrowth. A silk snag line. She froze, easing away from it while pushing Tam behind her, guiding him away from things he could no longer see with the naked eye in the failing light.

Traps, her fingers said. *Follow me.*

Tam grimaced in apology.

Hand on his elbow, she got him as close as she dared to the heart of the nest and pulled him to a stop. He stooped and chose a stick from the litter on the forest floor. Once again, the stick with its woolsey flag sailed over the web. The lacy fronds in the heart of the nest shivered.

Tam pushed her back. They retreated until he tugged her to a halt ten paces back. He picked up a short, heavy branch and pulled one of the leather laces from the depths of a thigh pocket and began wrapping it carefully around the middle of the branch.

Something moved under the ferns in the heart of the web complex. Cheobawn shuddered. By the Goddess, she hated spiders.

A high pitched, excited whistle caught at her heart and made her forget spiders and webs and stingers.

There was no mistaking the sound of a fuzzy gang on the hunt. The teaching videos did not do it justice. The high thin sound echoed eerily off the trunks of the trees, disguising numbers and exact direction. All the animals of the mountain knew this sound. It was meant to act as a goad, driving prey before them until the target gave up or ran until it's heart burst from exhaustion. Few willingly chose to die the death of a thousand bites. The little fuzzies relied on this and used it effectively in their hunting strategies.

Cheobawn looked anxiously into Tam's calm face. Time was running out for them. He was busy knotting the second leather lace to the end of the first. Stepping away from Cheobawn, he set it into motion, spinning the branch by its leash above his head until the air hummed with its passage. At just the right moment, he let it go. Branch and lace arced through the air and fell, landing with a loud thump in the center of the nest.

Cheobawn was not prepared for the violent reaction that followed. A dozen enormous black orbs the size of a fernhen rose out their dens and scurried about upon a tangle of legs as long as her arm. Horror sucked the air out of her lungs. She knew a stinger as long as her hand lay hidden under the belly of the heavily armored insect, sharp enough to pierce the toughest hide, long enough to penetrate the thickest fur. She shoved a fist in her mouth to keep from screaming and stumbled backwards.

Something dark darted at her from under the ferns near her feet. She did not have time to react, but suddenly Tam was there, catching her up by the collar of her tunic to jerk her away as he buried the blade of his stick in the center of the black body, pinning it to the ground. The spider's legs scrabbled for purchase in the soft duff. It was still trying to push its broken carapace towards her even as it died. Cheobawn moaned, unable to contain her horror any longer. Tam wrenched his weapon free and leaped away, pulling her with him. Dark blood flowed freely from the wound and the spider shuddered and died.

Death washed the ambient, a fierce thing that drowned out all else. Cheobawn felt it and in feeling it, could not shake it loose from her mind. She tried to keep it out but she had borrowed too heavily from the flesh of the mountain and Bear Under the Mountain relished death as much as it rejoiced in life. She had no power to resist his fierce pleasure at the spider's passing.

Tam signed something. She could not make her mind understand the flurry of fingers.

Tam bent down and caught at her chin, bringing his face close so that all else was blocked from her vision.

"We are almost there, wee bit," he whispered desperately. "Keep it together. Just for a few more minutes. Take us home."

Cheobawn blinked. His eyes were her lifeline. She reached out and touched his cheek. That touch was everything. His need for her, his need for her Good Luck washed through her, pushing Bear out of her mind.

She nodded. "Home," she said.

Tam smiled grimly and grabbed her hand, the strength of his grip grinding her bones together as he jerked her around and forced her to follow. The pain gave her focus. She got her feet under her and scrambled frantically to keep pace.

They ran. She struggled against the fear and the pain, trying to gather up the threads of their life once more. Bear Under the Mountain danced under her feet, death running like a fire across its pelt. *Live or die,* it whispered, *just remember, I keep what I take.*

Cheobawn tried to close her mind to its influence, but she needed to steal its flesh to keep on running and that flesh came at a price.

The rest of the Pack was where they had left them, though Megan was tugging desperately on Connor's arm, trying to get him moving. Connor ignored her, intent on their back trail. His face lit up with relief as Tam and Cheobawn came crashing through the underbrush. Alain, standing a little bit further on, waited patiently on them all.

Cheobawn waved them on, not bothering with the niceties of fingersign anymore and having no breath left to scream at them.

"Run!" Tam roared at them, furious that they had disobeyed his order. The sound echoed through the stillness of the twilight forest, marking them to any who could hear. It did not matter. Their retreat could not get any more chaotic than it already was.

Connor turned and ran, hard and fast, hand in hand with Megan, gathering up Alain as they passed him. The burst of speed would not last, Cheobawn knew. Though they had rested, she had pushed them beyond the limits of themselves all day. It would take more than a few moments rest to recover their full strength.

Tam let go of her hand as they caught up with the others and moved to Alain's side. Already Alain's pace faltered. She glanced at the red-haired boy's face as she ran beside him. His eyes were barely open, the motion of his legs oddly loose and disjointed. Tam put a hand on Alain's elbow as he ran beside him, guiding him over the rough ground.

Cheobawn risked another peek into the ambient. A many-headed monster raced at their heels. They were too close. Spurred on, she raced into the lead and picked up the pace, mercilessly asking her Pack to keep up.

When her feet landed on the packed earth of a wide trail, she very nearly missed it. She spun in a circle, disoriented by its sudden appearance and not sure which way to run.

Something flashed in the corner of her eye. She turned and stared in wonder. Lights. It could be only one thing. The Fathers had turned on the spotlights above the East Gate. Her knees went weak with her relief. They were nearly there.

She waited for her Pack, pushing each one towards the lights as they burst through the undergrowth and into the clear. Tam came last, behind Alain, who—through some miracle—was still on his feet.

A high-pitched squeal of something dying cut through the still air, then another and another.

Cheobawn looked up and met Tam's eyes. Their trap had been sprung but it would be too much to hope that the spiders would kill all the fuzzies. She tugged frantically at Alain's arm while Tam did the same on his side. They ran but their pace was maddeningly slow.

Disaster struck. Alain went down on his hands and knees. Tam cursed and stopped to help him up. Cheobawn reached down to help.

"Run!" Tam shouted, shoving her hands away. Cheobawn fell back, surprised by his hot fury. Tam grabbed Alain by the belt and hauled him to his feet, getting little help from Alain. Cheobawn grabbed Alain's belt on her side and between the two of them, they managed to get him running again. Ahead of them, Connor tugged frantically at the faltering Megan.

"No, no, do not stop!" Cheobawn screamed at Megan. "You are not safe yet. Run, run!"

Megan glanced back at Cheobawn, a desperate grimace on her face but the older girl managed to find some hidden reserve inside herself and sped up again. Connor ran at Megan's side encouraging her to pick up the pace. Somehow, she did. They raced together, down the trail.

A high pitched whistle rose up from the undergrowth not far behind them. The fuzzies were back on the scent trail. Alain needed no other goad. He shook their hands off and ran un-aided, Cheobawn and Tam still hovering at his side, watchful. The adrenaline would only take him so far.

They broke out of the tree line and staggered down the lane between the fields. The sky was gloriously scarlet with the last rays of the sun. Cheobawn nearly laughed in relief.

Alain stumbled, catching his toe on nothing. He managed to right himself, but after that his gait was less a jog and more a lurching hobble. Tam pulled Alain's arm over his shoulder and they ran on, Cheobawn guarding their back.

The whistling stopped, replaced by a restless chittering. The ravenous little eating machines hesitated just at the edge of the fields, confused by the Mothers' psi wards that protected the dome and all its surrounds. Cheobawn stopped and turned, taking a tighter grip on her hook. As she did, her left arm brushed the hilt of Alain's hunting knife where it still hung on her belt. She had forgotten it was there.

Cheobawn slid the long blade out of its sheath and gripped

it awkwardly. She knew nothing of knife fighting. It had not occurred to her that she would ever need the skill. Now she cursed her ignorance.

She held it out in front of her but it seemed to be in the way of her hook so she reversed it, holding the blade so that the edge faced outward to guard her left forearm, like armor. Satisfied, Cheobawn looked toward their backtrail, trying to stay calm. The wards would not hold against a gang in a hunting frenzy. The scent trail was too hot in their noses.

Tam took note of her absence at his side. "What are you doing?" he yelled, stopping.

"Run! Get them home. You need time. I will give you that," Cheobawn shouted. Alain did not hesitate. He turned and hobbled towards the gate as fast as he could. Tam stood his ground.

"I will stay and guard our back. Go help Alain," shouted Tam furiously.

"I cannot carry Alain but I can fight," Cheobawn said, her voice calm.

"You don't need to do this. We can make it. All of us. Together."

"Go!" Cheobawn screamed at him. Things shifted in the ambient. Blood lust outweighed caution. The fuzzies were coming.

"You should probably not argue with a Little Mother when she has her back up," drawled Zeff as he stepped out of the maize, his pair of boar hounds close on his heels, Sigrid following after. They were both well-armored and well-armed, long swords in both hands. Even the hounds had spiked collars around their vulnerable throats.

Cheobawn crushed the relief that threatened to overwhelm her. She had no time for it. She shoved it down into the black hole in her soul along with all the other soft and vulnerable parts of herself. Bear Under the Mountain had given her a taste of death. She meant to deal it in kind. Tam should have run when he had the chance. Now it was too late.

Things moved in the maize.

The hounds growled softly but stayed to heel, watching Zeff in anticipation.

Cheobawn took a step away from the men, giving her blade clear space to swing.

"You know what's out there, don't you?" Zeff commented softly, somewhere close behind her left shoulder. Veteran of many a close battle, she trusted that he would keep clear of the range of her blades.

"Fuzzies. A spider or two. They do not like the dogs, but it will not stop them from coming."

"No, it never does," agreed Zeff. "How many, do ya think?"

"Small fuzzy gang. The spiders got half. Maybe eighteen or twenty, at the most," she said, trying to track them all as they circled around her. "Maybe a half dozen spiders."

"Spiders and fuzzies. All at once. You surpass yourself, Little Mother," Zeff said with a small laugh.

"We have given them my scent. You can take Tam and Alain to safety. They will not follow you."

"Where would be the fun in that?" Zeff said softly. He put two fingers in his mouth and let out a piercing whistle. The boar hounds leapt into the air and raced into the maize, roaring in pleasure. A fuzzy squealed and died and then another. A spider darted out of the maize at her, whether to attack or merely flee-ing the sharp teeth of the hounds, she could not tell. Her hook sliced it in half, the parts tumbling past her as she stepped over them.

"Back up a bit, Little Mother. Let the dogs do their job,"

suggested Zeff. Cheobawn could not fault the logic of that. She retreated, checking her surroundings with a quick glance. Sigrid's blade was bloody, as was Tam's. Beyond, under the glare of the dome lights, Alain had gained the safety of the gate supported by Phillius. He joined Megan and Connor, who had been caught up in the arms of the crowd of Elders who stood behind the safety of the gates.

Looking back towards the maize, she realized her eyes could only see the after image of the lights. A stupid mistake, that. She blinked hard, desperately trying clear her vision. In that moment a shadow launched itself from the top of a maize stalk, aiming for her throat. Zeff's blade cut it out of the air. The fuzzy dropped to the dirt at her feet, its lifespark gone, now nothing but a bit of bloody fur. She steeled her mind against the ambient, letting death's dance take it without needing to watch. Peering about her for the next assault, she held herself ready.

Her eyes played tricks with the shadows as the glow in the western sky faded. She felt the handful of fuzzies—their intention a pressure wave against the walls around her mind—before she saw them, but it was already too late. Teeth and claws sank into the heavy hide of her boots and scrabbled ineffectually at her woolsey gaiters. One launched itself higher. She could not get her hook around in time so she batted wildly at it with her left arm. It squealed in pain, finding sharp steel instead of flesh, and tumbled away from her. Zeff finished it with a quick blow. The rest fell beneath her hook. Her blade hummed as she spun it through the air, its edge slicing through their brain pans like butter. She stamped her feet to shake off the remains, dislodging jaws that still bit even in death.

Backing away, her eyes searching the shadows, she put distance between herself and the smell of carnage, her hook held high.

Nothing more came out of the maize. She stood, her body taught, ready, unmindful of the blood running down the handle of her hook to drip from her knuckles. She dared a quick check of the ambient. Too many deaths swirled there, making her blind.

The baying of the dogs marked their path as they ran down the last of the predators. Soon, the maize field was empty, the sound of the hunt growing faint. She smiled as she listened to Sigrid whooping fiercely as he trailed close behind the dogs, finishing off the wounded. His joy, as simple and innocent as that of the hounds, was infectious, an intoxicating pulse that tugged at the fabric of her being. She imagined herself as a wild creature, free to run under the night sky, to howl at the stars and tear at the throats of all who wished her harm.

A harsh bugle shattered that spell. Zeff had his horn to his mouth, recalling the hunters. She shivered as the weight of her own small life crashed back into her mind, filling the void. For the first time since the glasslizard grove, she remembered she was just a little girl like every other little girl in the world.

Just for a moment, as her heart fluttered in her chest, her vision flashed to gray. She reached for the ambient but found nothing. Dismay filled her. Was there a limit to how long one could run on borrowed flesh? She could hear Mora in the back of her mind, scolding her for being so foolish.

Cheobawn shook her head to clear her vision or perhaps to clear her mind of the ghost voices. She looked around. The bright coppery smell of blood hung heavy on the still night air. What now? Was it done? What came next? She looked back at Tam. Her alpha slumped where he stood, his bladed stick planted in the soil like a staff. He leaned heavily into it, as if it were the only thing holding him up. Perhaps feeling her gaze, he lifted his head and met her eyes. There was no victory in that look, nor any triumph in his face. The clever boy full of strategies and logic, the fierce boy who played to win, this boy was gone. Only exhaustion remained. They still lived, but the game had pushed him beyond the place where it seemed to matter. It was done, his eyes told her.

So, she thought, with a soft sigh. *The sun can set, the moons can rise, and the forest can go back to being no fit place for human, man or child.* Best of all, the lives of four children no longer rested on her next move.

Cheobawn let go of it all, remembering too late to keep just enough energy to get her safely home and into bed.

The world swirled around her, the ground tilting under her feet.

Bear Under the Mountain harrumphed grumpily, its mood caught somewhere between pleasure and disappointment.

Are you not pleased? she asked it.

The mountain bear twitched its great pelt as the blood of spider and fuzzy drained down into the earth to join the rivers of blood that coursed hot and thick there under the surface. She flinched from that answer.

You did not kill us, she whispered defiantly. *We beat you, fairly.*

Bear smiled a canny smile and closed his eyes, content to wait.

Cheobawn did not remember hitting the ground.

Chapter Twelve

Cheobawn slept the clock around and woke ravenous. The Mothers fed her, giving her only broth and bread. She did not complain, eating most of it before falling back into a deep sleep.

On the second day, they gave her a rich stew. She managed to eat two bowls full before her stomach protested. Amabel consulted with the other healers and then reluctantly let her get out of bed, annoyed that Cheobawn seemed so healthy. She tottered from bed to lavatory and back again, bent over like an ancient oldma, trying to work the stiffness out of her muscles. She did not complain about this or her sore feet or the twinge in her knee. It seemed a reasonable price to pay for such a hard won foray.

The next morning Mora's wives all agreed that she might get better faster if she went back to her old routine, so Mora sent Cheobawn off to classes. The other children stared at her and whispered behind their hands, which was nothing new. The teachers were kind and considerate and attentive where they had never been before. She fled them all as soon as she could, hiding in the tubegrass plantings on the edge of the playground at recess. Megan did not come to school that day. There was a new helper, a woman whose belly was just showing the hint of a baby bulge, who sat in the shade a lot and did not know to come looking for her under the grass when the return bell rang.

Cheobawn waited for everyone to leave and then she curled up on the cool earth and fell asleep.

She opened her eyes to something tickling her nose and found Tam squatting beside her, caressing her face with a grass stalk. She stared at him sadly.

"You did not come," she said accusingly.

"We tried. We went to the infirmary, but Amabel said no and then we went to your apartment but Mora said no and today, before weapons drills, Hayrald said absolutely not, so here we are anyway," Tam said.

And here they all were, indeed. She looked up and found Megan, Connor and Alain looking at her over Tam's shoulders, anxious and concerned. She surprised herself by not being annoyed at their attention, as she had been with Mora and the Coven and Da and all the teachers.

Cheobawn sat up, drinking in the sight of them as she brushed the grass clippings from her hair. They all looked thinner. Alain's knee was in a plasteel brace. Connor's foot had been shoved into an adult slipper to accommodate the bandages. Megan had deep shadows under her eyes. Worry lines seemed to have permanently etched themselves into Tam's ten year old face, making him seem less beautiful but more wise.

Cheobawn noticed something else. Megan wore new clothes. Her shorts were muddy brown and the tunic a dusky green, identical to the boys' clothes. This explained Megan's absence on the playground. Megan had officially declared her Pack status. Her time was no longer her own. From now on she would study, train, and work alongside her Packmates. Cheobawn tried hard not to be sad at the change.

"I thought you were mad at me," she said softly.

"What? Why would we be mad?" Tam laughed.

"You saved us," Alain reminded her.

"You were amazing," Megan added.

Cheobawn shook her head.

"I messed up. I nearly got you killed about a million times. I forgot too many things. Important things. I forgot that a Pack works together and takes care of each other. And then at the end, I totally forgot the most important part."

"What part?" Tam asked, puzzlement warring with amusement on his face.

"I was so busy worrying about the big scary things out in the woods that I totally forgot about the scary things at home. What did you tell Hayrald?"

Alain shook his head, smiling in amazement, he and Connor exchanging knowing looks.

"That was one of the things we came over here to ask you," Tam said. "You first. What did you tell Hayrald?"

"Nothing," Cheobawn said. "I was afraid to talk to him, so I didn't. Or Mora either."

Connor laughed out loud and slapped Alain on the back.

"Told you," he crowed. "You owe me."

Tam looked a little concerned.

"I am afraid to ask. When you say nothing, you mean you did not tell them anything about our foray, right?"

"No," Cheobawn said, shaking her head, "I pretended I forgot how to talk."

The older children looked at each other and burst into howls of laughter.

"What is so funny?" asked Cheobawn, frowning.

"You," Megan said. "You have Mora and Amabel and Hayrald walking around thinking you are as fragile as eggshell."

"Yeah," Connor added, "they are all mad at us, like we broke you or something."

"We should come up with a good lie," Cheobawn suggested, deeply concerned that they had born the brunt of her bad decisions for three whole days.

"That leads me to the other thing we needed to ask you," Tam said. "Do you still want to be a part of our Pack?"

Cheobawn felt the hard little ball of sadness inside her chest begin to melt.

"Yes, please," she said from the bottom of her heart.

"Good, because we have a foray report to write," Tam said, pulling a form out of his pocket and unfolding it, "and it's already days overdue. Phillius is going to have my liver for breakfast if I don't get something down in writing by the end of the day. You are the only one who can help me."

Cheobawn smiled, happier than she ever remembered being. This was Tam; business first, niceties after. Cheobawn crawled out of her bower to look at the map printed on the report form, hungry to see its curved lines and precise labels. Truth be told, she had locked the memories of the journey away, unwilling to deal with them on her own. They were beginning to blur like a half-remembered dream. She was losing track of what had been real and what she had imagined while deep within the arms of Bear Under the Mountain.

"Why have you waited so long to write your report?" Cheobawn asked, curious.

"Because, Little Mother, after being interrogated almost non-stop for the past three days, singly and as a group, by just about every Elder in the village, we have all come to the same conclusion," Tam said brightly, "Not one of us has a clue as to what happened out there."

"You were there," Cheobawn reminded them all.

"Yeah, well, about that ..." drawled Alain.

"See, between being sick and scared and totally lost, none of us has been able to draw a clear picture of where we were and what we did," Tam explained.

"You changed direction so often, I was pretty sure we were going in circles," Connor nodded.

"The Elders keep treating us like we are hysterical little kids who saw a crawler under the bed," snorted Alain in disgust.

"It's embarrassing," agreed Connor.

"It would be nice to get points for the kills, too," Megan added. "Partial points for a fuzzy gang and a stinging spider nest would put us at the top of the first year pack standings."

"Never mind that, now. That's another battle. Let's start from the beginning," Tam said, patting the map.

The other children squatted around it and leaned in close to get a better view. Their fingers traced the line of the outward journey, along the East Trail, to the turn up the North Fork Trail, to the spot where they left the trail and cut through open country. They all generally agreed with the time and place referents that Tam guessed at. Megan remembered the place where they saw the fernhen. The tubegrass grove lay just uphill from the place on the map where the blue line marked the stream as it flowed down the mountain. This was all they were certain of.

The path of the return journey brought heated debate. They all agreed on the initial direction away from the spring but none of them could remember the time of day. Cheobawn could not help them. Time seemed to play tricks in her head. What had seemed like hours must surely have only been minutes, what seemed like forever had only been hours.

After much discussion, they used Connor's estimate. He seemed the most certain. Megan unsealed one of the deep pockets in her shorts and pulled out a tablet. A handful of colored styluses emerged from another. She began writing the map coordinates down the page in a column and putting the rough time estimates next to them. Tam made a small mapper's ruler appear from one of his many pockets, grabbed a stylus from Megan and began tracing the bits they were sure of on the map, placing the numbered boxes in the spots to mark the things they remembered.

Cheobawn sat back and watched them for a moment, a soft smile on her face. There was a new found confidence in their interactions, as if being a declared Pack made everything right in the world. They were like rocks rolling downhill now. The momentum of their trust that the world would give them what they needed crushed all resistance. Their belief was absolute, almost magical.

Magic. Cheobawn understood magic. Magic was merely the unknown, a wild thing undefined by logic or reason. By that thinking, surely she was not Bad Luck, but Good, undefined.

The ball of pain inside her eased a bit more.

Tam looked up and caught her smiling at him. He grinned back and returned to his argument with Connor about the distance of the first leg of their journey. Cheobawn leaned forward to joined in.

It took them almost two hours and much disagreement. At last Tam sat back to admire their work. Megan was still writing furiously, content with the tabulation on her paper. Connor ran his finger down the line etched on the map and tisked softly.

"Did you know you were doing this or was this all an accident?" he asked, bemused.

"What do you mean?" Cheobawn asked. Tam looked down, curious as well.

"You crossed the bhotta's path here and the direction change towards the spiders is here. The whole time we were running we were boxed in between the cliffs and rock slides and the bogs and marshes that make the East Road split off and veer south. The only way out was the way you led us. You were headed towards the South Road, weren't you?"

"We would have made it, too," Tam said, "if it weren't for the fuzzies."

Cheobawn looked at the map and the vague impressions and blurry images from that day began to make sense. She shrugged.

"I did not have a plan when we left the grove. I never had a plan. It was only towards the end that I realized where we were headed."

"I don't care how her Luck works, I'm just glad it does," Alain said fervently. Tam nodded.

"Wait," Megan said, "We're not done. Now that we have figured out the facts, we have to decide what to tell the Elders."

The Pack grew silent, somber looks on their faces. Cheobawn suddenly felt exhausted. Discovering the truth had taken all her powers of recall. Covering it up again seemed too daunting.

Tam studied their map and then looked up with a mischievous smile on his face.

"You know what I am thinking?" mused Tam, running his fingers over the map. "I'm thinking we tell them the truth."

"What? You mean turn this in as our foray report?" Megan asked aghast, as she waved her tablet in the air.

"It's too crazy," Alain said. "Nobody will believe it."

"Exactly," crowed Tam. "Give them a report they don't expect. It will take them weeks and weeks to decide if it is true or not and then weeks more to decide what to do about it."

A handful of weeks seemed like forever. Too far away to worry about. They all grinned in delight at Tam's brilliant plan.

Cheobawn laughed at Tam's logic but admitted, in the end, that it was faultless.

Chapter Thirteen

Hayrald was waiting for her at the end of the school day. Cheobawn paused on the top step when she saw him, uncertain of his mood and the reasons for him standing there with all the other waiting Elders. He was First Prime. He usually delegated his waiting time to his lieutenants. His presence surely could not have been out of concern. She had not needed an escort home from school since she was a little kid.

"Father," Cheobawn greeted him solemnly.

"Little Mother," said Hayrald, matching her formal address. He held out his hand and, after a moment's hesitation, she took it. They turned and walked down the promenade. She wondered where he might be taking her. It was certain her teachers had carried the tale of her miraculous recovery of language. Perhaps it was her turn to sit in front of the panel of inquisitors and suffer their questions. But no. He turned the corner and led her towards home.

"I understand Tam brought his Pack to see you today."

Cheobawn listened to the ambient, trying to tell if he was angry. It was as if Hayrald did not exist there. His control was impeccable. Her mother had chosen him as her Prime for a reason, after all. She would have to hunt out his feelings the hard way.

"Do not punish him for disobedience. It was needful," she said.

"Was it?" he said, his tone betraying nothing.

She considered many responses, struggling against the unfamiliar silence between them. This was Da, the holder of her deepest, darkest secrets. Had one simple foray outside changed all that? She retreated inside herself to think about that for a moment, trying to stay calm. It was in that calm place that she found her answer. There were things so indelibly etched into the ambient that even if all else turned to dust and blew away, these things would remain. The feelings between her and her Da were one such thing.

With a new sense of confidence she dared probe at something that was bothering her.

"Mother's job is very difficult, isn't it?" she said.

"Why do you think so?" Hayrald asked, undeterred by the sudden change of subject.

"No one yells at her when she makes a mistake."

"And you think this is bad?"

"I used to think it was a very good thing."

"But not anymore?" asked Hayrald.

"No. I think it makes her lonely."

Hayrald inhaled sharply, just like when he moved too fast and the old injury made his knee freeze up. Cheobawn caressed the back of his hand with her thumb, trying to comfort him.

"She has her Coven and me and the rest of her husbands," Hayrald said when he found his breath again. It was not a true answer to her question. She left it alone. Grownups could be very cagey when it came to certain subjects.

"Tam turned in our foray report today." she said, turning the conversation back to its beginning.

"I read it." Da said.

"Did you?" That was quick, she thought. "What did you think?"

"It was a very, um, interesting read." Hayrald said diplomatically. "The parts left out were more interesting than the parts left in. When did you learn to channel chi to enhance your strength? It is only taught in Temple. To twelve-year-olds. Have you been spying on the training sessions there as well?"

"What is chi?" Cheobawn asked, surprised that stealing life from Bear Under the Mountain was taught at all. Could other people see Bear? Why had no one ever told her?

"Ah," Hayrald breathed. "I thought as much. Yes, yes, a very informative read, that report."

"Do you think so? It seemed a little confusing. I thought we could have done better," she said, but she did not know if she meant the report or the experience it was based on. Perhaps it was both.

"We all learn from our mistakes. Next time you will remember your mistakes and not repeat them," her Da said sagely.

Next time. The words seemed like a promise. Da was not going to stop her if she wanted to go outside again.

Cheobawn smiled and pressed the back of his hand to her cheek. Da never made promises he could not keep.

Glossary

Alpha: A First. The dominant male or female in a group. The leader.

ambient: The communal psychic cloud surrounding all things.

Battle Trail: A sophisticated game of Dancing Molly, done in silence using fingersign. Used by the foray Packs and patrols.

Bear Under the Mountain: The synergistic sentience of all life north of the Escarpment. The persona given by Cheobawn to her perception of all planetary life as being a coherent, cohesive amalgam of the energies created by the interaction of said life.

bennelk: The smaller mountain cousin to the fenelk, these horned and tusked antelopes are the domes' riding animals for patrols and battles.

bhotta: Large, wingless lizard, dominant predator of the High Reaches.

black bead: A failed Ear whose psi is suspect and whose gift is not to be trusted. They are forced to wear a black stone in their omeh to mark their status. Most are killed outright on their third birthday.

blackoak: Wet loving tree with black bark and large, serrated and lobed leaves.

bloodstone: A gemstone prized by the domes for its range of colors, its hard crystalline structure, and its use as a psychic enhancer.

blue tag: Permission tag given to Packs to foray outside the dome.

buzzer: Large winged insect.

cedar: Ancient old growth tree with shredded bark and primitive leaves similar in form to Terran cedars.

Central Plaza: The plaza under the apex of the dome.

Choosingday: The day three year old girls must prove their psi abilities. Presented with two boxes, one containing something deadly, one containing a toy, the child must pick the correct one.

click: The distance a human man can walk in an hour.

Coven: The First Mother and all her wives.

croakers: Tiny, ground dwelling lizards.

Dancing Molly: Child's game of follow the leader.

demi-Pack: Provisional Packs. Experimental and sometimes temporary arrangements, they are the first packs formed by children over the age of eight.

dubeh leopard: Large black cat-like predator.

Ear: Female member of a Pack. A psi adept.

East Trail: The road leading out the East Gate.

Elder: Tribal member over the age of sixteen.

Escarpment: The southern boundary of all tribal land.

fenelk: Horned and tusked antelope from the southern forests, it is largest herbivore north of the Escarpment.

fernhen: Large ground nesting bird prized for its eggs. A seed eater.

First Mother: The dominant Mother in the Dome hierarchy, ultimately responsible for all life in and around the Dome.

First Prime: First Husband of the First Mother and her Coven. Dominant Father in the Dome hierarchy.

flutterflies: Tiny, winged lizards.

foray form: A detailed topographic map of the area around the dome updated daily by the Elders to include current threats. The Packs use them to plot out their intended routes and missions.

fuzzy gang: Small, communal-minded predator as large as a child's fist

gaiters: Leather thorn guards. Part of what is considered light armor.

glasslizard: Glider lizard with transparent skin. Not a true flier.

gorgeberry: Small fruit bush with golden berries.

grunter: Herbivore about the size and weight of a man that lives in the needletree forests. Sharp tusks are used for digging up fungus balls and bulbs.

High Mother: The leader of all the domes in the High Reaches, voted into office by the First Mothers of each dome.

hopper: Small, ground-dwelling marsupial.

Little Father: Formal title of boys who have not reached their majority.

Little Mother: Formal title of girls who have not reached their majority.

longpine: Giant needletree with extremely long needles.

Maker of the Living Thread: Master Geneticist and Healer. Amabel, Mora's Second wife, is the Maker for Windfall Dome.

needletree: Dry-loving tree that grows on the lower slopes of the mountains.

Natalmother: Mother who is impregnated by the Maker of the Living Thread and who bears the risk of gestating a child to full term.

Nestmother: The Mother in charge of rearing a group of children between the ages of three and seven (if male), and three and eight (if female). After the age of seven boys are traded, and after the age of eight girls join Packs.

North Fork Trail: Northern branch of the trail that splits from East Trail to run along the top of the cliffs and scree slopes above the bogs.

oldma: A female who has retired from the politics of running the dome.

oldpa: A male too old to ride patrol.

omeh: The plasteel and bloodstone necklace containing the genetic map of the wearer worn by every human north of the Escarpment. A collar woven whole around the necks of every child not long after their birth, the pattern of which is unique to each dome.

Orchard Road: North road leading past the orchards into the north paddocks.

Orchard Trail: Road leading out the North Gate.

Pack Hall: Residence where the declared Packs live in their dorm rooms.

Pack: A group formed by children. It is a requirement of any who want to leave the dome. To Pack is enter into a formal binding contract with a chosen few. Upon reaching majority, these ties become permanent, the members then considered Husbands and Wives.

Pantry: The dome's communal food storage.

piper: Small, ground nesting bird that eats mostly insects.

plasteel: A generic term used to refer to any form of extruded plastic. Made from plant material, it has the tensile strength of tungsten-enhanced steel.

Psi: Short for psionic. The genetically bred abilities of dome women to perceive the world using super-psychic means.

red tag: Foray tag that grants permission for outside travel. Used to track all dome dwellers who have gone outside.

Son of the Flesh: Boys born of the dome in which they reside.

Son of the Heart: Boys traded in Trade Fairs as future Husbands to the Mothers of the recipient domes.

South Road: The road that splits from the North Fork Trail and goes south and then east, to run along the southern edges of the bogs.

spidersilk: This refers to the thread made from the silk of a small, golden spider and also to the fabric woven from this thread. Twice as strong as plasteel, weight for weight.

squeaker: Small forest frog.

sugarsip: Parasitic tree plant with sweet nectar in their flowers.

treebear: Giant, clawed marsupial standing man-tall at the shoulder. An opportunistic feeder, it can digest bone and most plant fibers.

treehoppers: Large, arboreal marsupial.

Truemother: A term of deep respect and honor given to the Mother whose egg is used to conceive a child. Even after minor genetic manipulation, she is still considered the Truemother.

tubegrass: Tall bamboo-like tree.

underager: Children under the age of eight.

watercup: Parasitic tree fungus.

Waterfall Trail: Road leading out the South Gate.

wayfaring boots: Sturdy hiking boots, not worn inside the dome.

Weapons Locker: Building on the south side of the Central Plaza where the weapons and tools are stored.

Weapons Master: Elder in charge of Weapons Locker, this is a post taken in shifts by the more dominant males.

West Road: Road leading out the West Gate

woolsey: Spidersilk and wool fabric.

Rank & Dome Affiliation

Cheobawn: Female born in Windfall Dome, Mora is her Truemother, Nestmother, and natalmother. Black Bead in Tam's demi-Pack holding no rank. An Omega Ear.

Megan: Female born in Windfall Dome. Amabel is her Truemother. Alpha Ear in Tam's demi-Pack.

Tam: Male born in Waterwall Dome. Alpha male.

Alain: Male born in Firewalker Dome. Tam's Second.

Connor: Male born in Waterwall Dome, Tam's Third, Tam's Truebrother.

Phillius: Hayrald's Third. Husband to the Coven.

Sigrid: Alpha male to Ramhorn Pack.

Hayrald: First Prime. Mora's Fist Husband. Husband to the Coven, titular head of the Fathers of Windfall Dome.

Mora: First Mother to Windfall Dome. Alpha Ear of the Coven. High Mother to all the High Reach Domes. Truemother of Cheobawn.

Menolly: High Priestess to Windfall Dome, Mora's Fourth Wife.

Zeff: Packless oldpa.

Amabel: Mora's Second wife and Master Maker of the Living Thread.

Cheobawn's Adventure Continues in The Black Bead Chronicles:

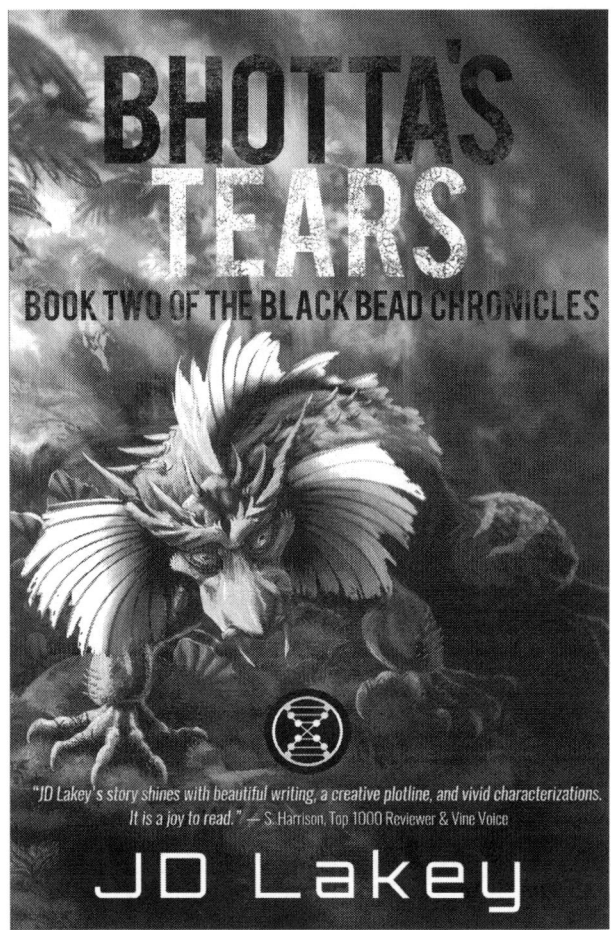

Bhotta's Tears:
Book Two of the Black Bead Chronicles

Something ominous has climbed the Escarpment and now wanders in the southern forests. Cheobawn and her pack must find it before the elders get wind of its presence and go hunting it with deadly intent.

The epic adventure that began with *Black Bead* continues in *Bhotta's Tears*. Journey along as Cheobawn, Megan, Tam, Connor, and Alain unravel the mysteries of their village under the dome.

About the Author

J.D. Lakey was born and raised on the high plains of Montana under an endless sky and as far from civilization as anyone in the twentieth century could get. There she explored the finer nuances of silence and the endless possibilities of the imagination. The stories were always there. The shifting of fortunes finally granted her the time to gather all the stories and give them flesh. An avid reader of science fiction and comics, she currently lives in San Diego, California where she divides her time between her writing, commuting on the I-5, and spending time with her family.

A Message from the Author

Dear Reader,

Thank you for reading! I hope you enjoyed *Black Bead: Book One of the Black Bead Chronicles*. This is a story I have been writing in various forms for the past twenty years and I'm pleased to finally be able to bring you the full story of Cheobawn. Many readers have written asking for more and I find the story continues to write itself, so I invite you to continue the journey along with Cheobawn in Book Two, *Bhotta's Tears*.

You are the reason that I keep writing and Cheobawn's story continues to be told. I'd love to hear what you liked about the stories, and yes, even what you hated. You can write to me at **info@jdlakey.com** and visit me online at **jdlakey.com** to sign up for my mailing list and read my quirky blog posts - no spamming, I promise! Just some periodic meanderings and giveaways. And don't forget to follow me on Facebook, Twitter, and Instagram under **@JDLakeyAuthor, @darkvstar,** and **JD.Lakey.Books**, respectively. I look forward to connecting!

Finally, I need to ask a favor. If you enjoyed this book, I'd love a review of *Back Bead* on Amazon or Goodreads. As an independent author, reviews are the single most important way to ensure that I can keep writing. The powers that be look at quantity and quality of reviews in deciding to support me. You, the reader, have the power to make or break a book.

Thank you again for reading, please keep in touch.

In gratitude,

Made in the USA
San Bernardino, CA
13 June 2017